TRIPLE ZINGER

JACKIE GRANGER

TO MY DAUGHTERS –

Linda: for encouraging me to dust off and finish the novel I started ten years ago; and, Patti: for designing the cover.

PROLOGUE

Connie O'Rourke pulled the belt of her trench coat tighter around her waist, adjusted the brim of her hat over one eye and looked furtively behind her. When she looked back at her reflection in the bedroom mirror, she said in a sultry voice, "Driver, take me to the CIA building. No. Lose the trench coat," she said as she took it off and laid it on the chair next to her dresser. "You look like you belong in a 1940's black and white movie, for crying out loud."

"But, the hat – now that's a different story," she smiled as she looked at herself again. She had been so excited when she found that cute, black fedora. She intended to wear it at least once during her long and illustrious covert career – perhaps while tailing Russian spies in Budapest or Berlin. But that was before she had her interview at the CIA.

"Connie, my girl, who the hell are you kidding? You are not going to be the world's greatest spy since Mata Hari. You're going to start work at the CIA tomorrow as a glorified secretary." She took off the hat and tossed it on her dresser.

She remembered how stunned she was when she had her interview and learned the only jobs open to women at the CIA were that of secretary and clerks. This is 1965, for crying out loud, she fumed. Yet the only career choices anywhere for women were that of teacher, secretary or nurse.

"So, you are going to use that G.P.A. of 3.7 and your degree in International Studies to type, to file, and to fetch coffee," she said softly to her image in the mirror. Tears started welling up in her eyes.

"Oh, phooey. Quit feeling sorry for yourself, kiddo," she whispered. "How many people in your graduating class are lucky enough to be working at the CIA?"

As far back as she could remember, she wanted to work for the CIA. She devoured spy novels from the time she learned to check out books at the library. When her friends were reading "Photo-play" and catching up on all the Hollywood gossip, Connie was off in the world of intrigue and mystery. Why such an unusual choice for a girl growing up in the fifties and sixties? Simple, her Dad. He was a policeman in the Boston Police Department. What else do you do if your name is Liam O'Rourke and you live in Boston?

When Liam, Lee now that he was on the Department, came home from work, he would share his day, not with her mother, who didn't want to hear about it, but with his daughter, Connie. His wife, Catherine, always felt if she didn't know about what Lee did at work, it would somehow keep him safe on the job. It wasn't that she didn't care about him. Lord, she was crazy about him. If something happened to Lee, her whole world would come to an end. So that's how she handled being married to a policeman.

"Lee," she would say, "please don't tell me what you do. I love you too much."

But, it wasn't her mother's world that came to an end. It was her father's. One day when Connie was in high school, her mother laid down on the sofa and fell asleep after complaining of a headache. She never woke up. She died of a massive stroke. Her father did not go to work for three weeks after his beloved Catherine died. He stayed in his room and did what the Irish are famous for. He drank and he cried. He spoke to no one, not even Connie.

She could still remember the unbearable silence that permeated the house during that time. But, the worst was when she could hear the uncontrollable sobbing coming from her father's room. It seemed to vibrate through the walls. It was then she would go to her room, get into bed and pull the covers over her head trying to block out the sound of the wailing. It never helped.

She would fix her father meals and leave them outside his door. More often than not, hours later, she would find the food still on the tray, untouched and cold. There was nothing she could do for him.

At the end of three weeks, Lee came out of his room. Connie was in the living room watching the Red Sox play the Yankees on T.V. She wasn't a fan of baseball, but she thought if she did something her father loved to do – watch the Red Sox – that would somehow bring her closer to him.

"Connie," he said in a thin, weak voice. At first she didn't hear him. He was so quiet. "Connie, my girl, God wouldn't take me."

With her eyes closed, she slowly turned toward the voice. When she opened them, her heart seemed to stop beating. There stood her once handsome, tall, Irish father, now stooped and shrunken. His thick, dark hair uncombed and unwashed seemed to be plastered to his skull. His eyes like hollow orbs were trying to focus and make sense of the world around him.

"Oh, Dad!!" she cried as she ran across the room to him. "I love you so much. I'll take care of you. Please don't be sad anymore. Please don't cry anymore. Please, Dad." The words came tumbling out as she threw her arms around his neck and hugged him.

The physical closeness of his daughter seemed to pour strength into him like electricity running its way through a lamp cord. His limp arms at his side now circled his daughter. He hugged her, slowly at first.

"I'm OK now, Connie," he said with a voice that began sounding like the Dad she knew. "You'll see, it will be all right, My love. Oh, Love, don't cry. I'm back now," he said as he wiped away the tears on her cheeks.

Thinking back on that time, Connie saw it from a different perspective – a mature perspective. "Dear God, let me find someone who will love me as much as my father loved my mother," she whispered on that June day in 1965.

JUNE 10, 1965 – TEL AVIV, ISRAEL

David Levi tossed his dirty T-shirts into his already filled suitcase. He had to sit on it in order to lock it. Hefting it off the bed, he took one last look at the room where he had lived for the past four years as a university student.

"Shalom, small room. Shalom, university. Shalom big city. I am off to fresh air, sun light, soft breezes and the lush fields of the kibbutz," he said softly as he stepped into the hallway and closed the door to that cramped, hot room for the last time. He was going home to his family where the entire kibbutz awaited him.

As he walked down the street to catch his bus, David was oblivious of the stares from the women, both young and old who passed him. He was taller than the average Israeli. With his dark hair, light hazel eyes and swarthy complexion, he was hard to miss. He wasn't textbook handsome, but there was something about him. The way he would cock his head when he listened or the way his smile would start from the corner of his mouth, it was enough to make young women want to go to bed with him and old women want to mother him. You would think he had few male friends – too much competition for them. But in truth, he had many friends both male and female. His easy going personality and his open friendliness made it hard not to like him.

He wasn't sorry to be leaving Tel Aviv. Most people found the city fascinating. It was new. It was the center of power here in Israel. There were things happening everyday of the week. But, to David, it was the countryside he needed. It was the soil that contained life not some steel and concrete building. After four grueling years at the University and two before that in the Army, he needed to get back to the countryside and restore his soul.

During his last year in school, he hadn't been home once, not even for a short weekend visit. He was always too busy with his studies or with the many friends he had met. But, now here he was, an agriculture degree in hand, finally going back – back to his roots where he was born and had lived for the first eighteen years of his life.

Two hours outside of Tel Aviv sitting on the bus taking David home, he began thinking about his parents. Oh, how he missed being with them this past year. The once a week telephone calls were no substitute for the warm embraces, the shared laughter, or the quiet evening conversations. Here he was almost twenty-five years old; and he still missed his family. He smiled at this thought. But the truth was his parents and sister Rachel were not only his family, they were also his friends. He knew what his father would do as soon as he walked in the front door – pull out the bottle of slivovitz. He always did. It was funny, his father hadn't lived in Yugoslavia for 30 years, since he was a young man actually, but he still maintained that the drink for all celebrations should be that horrible plum whiskey.

David's mother, who was from Hungary, and his father were both unusual in that they had come to Israel long before the Second World War. They were like the pioneers in America who lived in sod houses and fought the Indians. Only here when his parents came, they lived in the desert in tents for the first three years and the Indians weren't Indians – they were worse. They were the Arabs.

How many times had his parents told his sister and him the story about how they met. And, which story were they to believe? The one where the dashing and handsome young man named Benjamin swept the shy and quiet young girl, Sarah, off her feet. This was the one told by their mother. Or, should they believe the one told by their father? There was a young man on whom God smiled. He gave the slow-witted, humble Benjamin one of the most beautiful women in the entire country. Even though she had every unmarried man in the country as a suitor, she chose him. He and Rachel could never agree on which story they liked better. Twenty more minutes and he would be home.

All of a sudden David was thrown forward as the bus driver slammed on the brakes. The bus had just come around a turn on the side of a low-lying hill and run into a police roadblock. After getting the bus under control, but now facing the hill rather than the road ahead, the driver leaned out the window and yelled at the policeman at the barricade.

"What are you trying to do, get us all killed putting that roadblock so close to the bend in the road?" No one on the bus could hear what the middle-aged policeman said to the driver, but they did see the driver's face drain of all color.

"No!" thought David. "Something terrible has happened. Dear God, please don't let it be the kibbutz."

He was up out of his seat and running down the aisle. He had to know. He could not sit there any longer. The bus driver tried to stop him, told him to wait. But, David just roared, "Open the door, and do it now." Something in his face, the command of his voice made the driver do as David asked.

Once outside, David went after the first policeman he saw and grabbed his arm swinging him around. Instinctively, the policeman brought his Uzi up while reaching for the trigger of the gun. When he realized it was only a passenger from the bus, he broke into a torrent of angry words.

"What do you mean grabbing me? I could have killed you without thinking! Now get back on the bus before I . . . " That's as far as he got before David, without touching him further, leaned forward holding the policeman's gaze with his own said very quietly, "You will tell me what has happened."

"It's the kibbutz. It's been attacked!"

Even though the policeman had been in this job for fourteen years now, he found it difficult to go on. The bile was coming up in his throat. "Everyone has been killed. Everyone – men, women, even the children." It was then that the policeman began to weep.

"Who did it?"

"Who do you think?" the policeman shouted at him.

Again, David began to run. Amid the shouts to stop, not to go further, he ran. He had to see. He had to be sure.

For the rest of his life, no matter what he saw or what he did, nothing, nothing would ever be as bad as what he saw when he arrived at the parameter of the kibbutz – the blood, the mutilated bodies, but, above all the stench of death. And, nothing, nothing would ever alter the course of his life again the way the sight of his family and childhood friends lying lifeless in the hot sun did on that June day in 1965. Because, it was on this day David Karoly Levi joined the Mossad.

JUNE 10, 1965 – MOSCOW, SOVIET UNION

"Ah, Monsieur Le General," the old soldier said when he saw the young lieutenant, Nicholas Gregorovich enter the room.

Nicholas smiled at Ivan Petrovich, his father's army colleague from the Second World War. Ivan, in his turn, looked with such warmth into the face of the handsome young son of his old army captain. He felt duty bound to watch after this boy. He owed that to Nicholas' father. And, of course, when young Nicholas received any honor, it was because he, Ivan, had done such a good job of keeping the boy on the straight and narrow all these years.

They were standing at the entry gates to the military records archive deep in the bowels of the Army headquarters off Dzerzinsky Square. The room was buried so deep that even a nuclear bomb could not touch it. It seemed the Soviets made sure the world would never learn of the terrible atrocities committed in the glorious name of "Communism".

"And, how is life working for that dog, Polakova?" spat Ivan to the young man.

"Petrovich, my friend, you must be careful how you speak, even down here. And, my stepfather is fine this morning. Thank you for asking. Now before you start to tell me all your war stories, let me into the records, because I am here on official Soviet business," Nicholas said with a grin as he stood erect and tried to look important.

"Where would I find information on the old military campaign in Gdansk? A daughter of a former tank commander needs verification for her appointment to the University."

"You will find the file in Room D on shelf 12," Ivan said proudly. No other clerk in the archives had Ivan's memory for where everything was stored. Others had to look up the location of information in a directory, but Ivan with his unique photographic memory knew where every piece of history was located. Even the years and the hard drinking had not diminished that talent.

My father's old friend does not belong down here. He belongs with the historians in the academia writing a history of the Soviet Union, Nicholas mused as he went in search of Room D, shelf 12. But, maybe that is exactly why he is here. Ivan remembers the past clearly, and no one in the government wants to hear the truth about how they got there. If he wasn't such a lovable old bear with a brilliant war history in Leningrad, he would have been shot years ago. Unfortunately, that was one of the reasons vodka was so necessary in this country. One could be gifted and intelligent, but only gifted and intelligent in the areas the government wanted you to be, Nicholas thought as he entered Room D.

As with the usual Soviet mistrust, the young daughter of the military hero at Gdansk had to be checked out before her University professorship could be approved. Hopefully, her ancestors had not pissed on the wrong blade of grass, or she would be barred from every decent job for life.

"Ah well, on with the confirmation," Nicholas shrugged in resignation. This was the one part of his job he loathed. He was one of the top graduates of the Soviet Military Strategy Academy – the most prestigious military school in the Soviet Union, and here he was going through old, musty smelling records. Working for his stepfather did not mean curried favors as everyone else seemed to think.

Ten minutes later, he confirmed that yes, the future professor's father had a clean and flawless career, albeit short. He was killed as the German Panzers came to reclaim the Polish land back from the Russians – for what, the hundredth time over the centuries? As Nicholas was returning the file to the shelf, he noticed another file trimmed in red stuck in the back of the shelf. He knew that file should not be there. It should be in a locked room with entrance by written permission only. A file trimmed in red meant it was top-secret, eyes only.

"Ivan, whether a friend of my father's or not, you are going to hear about this," Nicholas fumed. He would quietly but very firmly tell Ivan about this terrible mistake and make sure nothing like this happened again. He wedged it out and checked to make sure the file was still sealed, no other papers had fallen out behind the shelf. It was then he saw the name on the file – Sergei Androvo Gregorovich. This was his father's file! What did his father ever do to end up in a secret file? Nicholas scanned the area to check for security cameras. Of course, there would be none in this room. No secret files were expected to be here. He carefully removed the black seal, fully intending to put it back when he finished reading it.

There was a letter addressed to Josef Stalin! His mother and father knew Stalin when they were young. They always said he would get to the top. But, they feared what would happen when he did.

Looking into his eyes at the emptiness was what made them hope someone would stop him before he got control. And, they were right. It takes emptiness to order the murder of twenty million of your own people. Stalin had wiped out so many people that entire languages were lost. And, he did it behind the "Iron Curtain", as Churchill had called it. The rest of the world did nothing to stop him. The British, the Americans, the Germans, they must have known what was happening. Yet, no one came. Everyone silently turned their backs and let the slaughter go on, and on and on.

Nicholas pulled out the letter and recognized the handwriting of his stepfather, Igor Polakova.

"Why would he be writing to Stalin?" Nicholas mused as he began to read it.

07 August 1945

My dear Comrade and old friend:

It is with a heavy heart that I must be the bearer of such terrible news. I have just learned our good friend (or the man we both thought was our good friend), Captain Sergei Androvo Grego-

rovich, has been corrupting some of our brave and honorable young soldiers. Oh, how can I possibly explain this most heinous atrocity to you except to be perfectly frank. Captain Gregorovich has been having homosexual relations with some of the men in our unit. There, I have said it, and even as I write, I am ashamed and as angry as you must be upon reading it. Your mind must be alive with loathing.

What must be done, I ask myself? Sergei, I do not even like to use his familiar name, is one of our country's heroes. He was with us at the beginning when we were young and had our dreams of the future. Yet, he has made a mockery of those dreams that you, dear Comrade, have made into glorious reality. The young men in my unit with whom he had relations, I will take care of myself. I would not trouble you with such insignificant problems as those at a time when the fate of the entire world is upon your shoulders. But, I come to you now regarding what must be done with Gregorovich.

Although Gregorovich is a dog and deserves a dog's death, he has a wife who is innocent of any wrong doing. She has served the State well. Ilena

Gregorovich too was with us from the beginning. She should not be tainted with her husband's sickness. If a trial is held with the truth told, then Ilena will be shunned forever for something for which she is completely free of blame. Therefore, dear comrade, may I make a proposal to you which I think will solve these many problems?

I will see to it that during our next confrontation with the hated Germans, Captain Gregorovich does not return alive. This will wipe out the cancer that has infested us here. Ilena and her young son, Nicholas will not be touched by this. However, I do think it would be wise that Ilena no longer retain her job within the government. Although innocent, it would be in our country's best interest.

If this is acceptable to you, please inform me. I will carry out everything as a servant of our country. You need no longer give thought to this.

Yours faithfully,

Nicholas stood absolutely still, but within him was a roar of such rage his mind could not even function. How long had he stood there – 10 seconds, 10 minutes, 10 hours, he did not know. Slowly his eyes focused, and he became aware of his surroundings.

"You son of a bitch. You were my parents' friend! My mother and father loved each other beyond words. Their worlds revolved around each other. What did you do, Igor, and why?" he thought wildly. There was only one person who could help him now, his mother.

"Oh, please my beloved mother let this be one of your lucid days when we can talk and you can remember what it is I ask of you. I need you now more than ever to be whole today, lovely Mother," he prayed.

Nicholas unbuttoned his shirt and stuffed the top-secret file under his tunic. His hands were shaking so badly. Three times he had to try to close the top button. He ran his hands over his face and his fingers through his hair. He wished there was a mirror in the room. He needed to be sure he looked calm when he walked out of here, because inside he was sure he was as close to madness as anyone could ever be. At this moment, he did not know if he would even be able to form words as he left. Hopefully, Ivan would be busy when he left and would not require more than a simple good-bye.

Somehow Nicholas arrived at his mother's house on the outskirts of Moscow. How he got there and which streets he drove to get there, he would never remember. He entered without knocking and was immediately struck by the memories of his childhood. Ilena was born in this house. Her father was a doctor and her mother a piano teacher at the gymnasium. She had two older sisters who had moved away with their husbands. So, when her parents died, the house became Ilena's. She never gave it up, even after Sergei was killed. When she married Igor and moved to an apartment in Central Moscow, she still retained the house. She kept it, because she wanted to be able to give something of herself to her son. It was highly unusual for an ordinary Soviet citizen to own a home. But, by the time she married Igor, he was high enough in the military that he could command favors. Now she had gone full circle. She was back here once more. Ilena was here as she waited for death to come.

Nicholas had remembered how solicitous Igor had been about having his mother live back here. "Perhaps her memory will come back if she is surrounded by the things of her past, Nicholas," Igor had told him after his mother had the second small stroke. Nicholas believed him then. He thought Igor was just as devastated as he was. But, now he knew better. Igor had simply wanted her out of the way. Out of his life now that she was no longer the beautiful Ilena. As he thought about it, he realized Igor had not come to visit his mother once since her birthday last February.

"That pig." If Igor had been standing next to him at this moment, Nicholas would have killed him.

When he entered his mother's room, he saw she was sitting in her chair looking out the window. The nurse who attended his mother got up to leave to give him privacy. As she passed him at the door, she whispered that things were about the same. It was then his mother turned her head and smiled.

"Oh, Sergei, my darling. You have come home so early today. What a pleasant surprise. I am so happy as always when you are here."

"No, Mother, it is just me Nicholas, your son," Nicholas said softly as he walked toward her chair. "Please, Mother, please know who I am," he screamed in his mind.

"Nicholas, of course. You look so much like your father. I was in a dream just now. And, then you came and became a part of that dream with me," she said as she stroked his face with her soft hand. "Have I told you how much I love you, My Son?"

Nicholas buried his face in her grey hair. "Have I told you how beautiful you are, My Mother?" he said as he drew back and looked into her dark eyes that seemed alert and knowing. He knew he didn't have much time before the curtain would fall again on her mind and the confused look would return.

"Mother, tell me about how you came to know Igor?" He could hardly keep his voice steady as he asked the question.

"Igor? I knew him as long as I knew your father. The three of us were at the University together. That was what I was dreaming about just now. The three of us were so young, so full of ideals and hope. I was going to be Russia's poet laureate, your father the editor of the newspaper, and Igor the supreme general of all the army. The innocents of youth," she said as she gazed out the window again.

"Mother, why didn't you marry Igor back then? Why did you marry my father if the three of you were so close?"

"Oh, Nicholas, there was never anyone else for me but your father. I was so in love with him. He was so handsome, just like you. He was tall with black hair and had that dashing mustache. But, it was in his eyes I saw the gentleness and laughter and trust that made me know my life had to be with him. Your father, I know, felt the same way about me. Igor never had that gentleness about him. He seemed to want to possess everything. Your father, he just wanted to embrace life – to feel life."

"You know, Nicholas, when Sergei was killed, I thought about killing myself as well. There just wasn't any reason for me to live anymore. I know I can tell you this now. You are a young man and can understand. I had you and I loved you, but when Sergei died, it seemed my life had been ripped in two and there was only half of me left standing."

"Then why did you marry Igor after my father died?" he asked quietly.

"Because I had no where to go. I had no money to take care of you. You see, Nicholas, after your father was killed, I lost my job in the Cultural Ministry and couldn't find work. It was like I was an outcast in my own country. I have never been able to understand that. I don't know what I did wrong."

"Nothing! You did nothing wrong, Mother," Nicholas said fiercely.

"Then when I barely had enough food left, one day Igor came and asked me to marry him. I had no choice. It was either that or starve. I know the marriage has been a disappointment to Igor. He expected me to love him as I did your father. I never did. I never could," Ilena said as she lay her head back in the chair and closed her eyes.

"I'm tired, Nicholas. Will you help me back to my bed?"

"Yes," he said simply.

"Sleep now, Mother. Go back to those happy dreams of long ago. I will come and see you tomorrow," he said as he helped her into the bed and pulled the blankets around her. She was asleep when he kissed her forehead in a farewell gesture.

Driving back into Moscow on that June day in 1965, Nicholas gripped the steering wheel so hard his fingers began to ache. "That fiend! How could he do that to my mother? How could he bring her so much pain? I will destroy you, Igor Polakova; the same way you destroyed my father," Nicholas shouted.

CHAPTER 1

"What? Are you crazy, Aaron? Absolutely not. I won't go. In fact, I quit," yelled David. "I joined the Mossad to fight the Arabs not screw some floozy secretary in Washington. And, since when is the Mossad in the pimping business? Answer me that." He was fuming as he paced around the office of his handler.

"David, David, David. Calm down. You will be fighting the Arabs but just in a different way," Aaron Zucker said quietly. "Look, you are so obsessed with revenge. Keeping you here is not a good thing. You are too emotional. And, that leads to mistakes we cannot afford. No, before you start to scream at me again, sit down and listen to me," he said as he held up his hand.

"We learned our lesson last month during the Six Days War with Egypt. When we asked for help from the United States as the bombs started falling, did they come? Did they help? No, we got nothing. And, information from the CIA blows hot and cold depending on whether the oil is flowing their way or not. We give them what we have and they give us *bupkus*. We are in this alone, David. The War proved that. We need to know what the Russians are up to. Who else but the Russians armed Egypt to the teeth? We know they are supplying money and arms to the Palestinians and the Syrians. Iraq looks like it is ready to fall. Someone is pulling the strings in those countries; and, we need to know who and what is going on. If the CIA won't cooperate, then we will go get their information from them ourselves. And, that is why we need you, dear boy.

"So, I am being sent to Washington to *schtupp* the CIA's Russian Desk secretary to get those secrets. Like a mere secretary would know any Russian secrets. You've got to be nuts, Aaron," David said with a sneer.

"I wouldn't put it so crudely, David.

"You are asking me to prostitute myself! How the hell would you put it?"

"Look, because of your Southern Slav background, you were at the top of your class in Russian language. You speak English brilliantly. You sailed through code breaking; almost put your instructor in the hospital in your unarmed combat classes; and, I hate to say this because you will get angry again – but you have charm. Tut, tut, tut," Aaron cut David off before he could say a word.

"Yes, charm. That is what we need. Right now, the Americans know every Mossad agent in the U.S. You, they don't know. You will be perfect. Until things settle down in the region, the CIA is very closed mouthed. If they are seen working with us, they are afraid the spigot will be shut off. We need answers now, David. If the Egyptians can launch an attack on us like they did in June, then all the other countries can catch us by surprise too."

"And, let me tell you about that mere secretary. Her name is Connie O'Rourke. She has a degree in International Studies and speaks Russian fluently. Consequently, her boss, Tom Bursak, trusts her completely. If he knows, then she knows. Very unusual for the CIA. We want you to get to know her. Take her out on dates. Find out what she knows about the Russian activities here in the Middle East. But, just to be clear - we don't require you to, ah, *schtupp* her. So, you see David, you will be fighting the Arabs – just not here in Israel."

"Well, what does this Connie O'Rourke look like?" David said somewhat mollified. "Some horsey woman with buck teeth, I bet."

"Actually, no. Here is her picture," Aaron said as he slid the photo across the desk. "In my opinion, she is quite attractive. But, what do I know? I'm just an old man who has seven grandchildren."

As David looked at the picture, he became quiet. Finally, he whispered, "She has hair like my sister, Rachel." He looked up with sorrowful eyes. "Aaron, am I ever going to be free of the nightmares?"

"Ah, *Boychick*. There aren't many of us here in Israel or many Jews around the world for that matter who don't have nightmares of their past – if not the Nazis then of the pogroms, and now the Arabs. It never ends, you know. I have always thought Abraham was a schmuck. Why didn't he just tell God to choose somebody else when he had the chance? Instead thousands of years later, here we are *God's chosen people* who have been paying for it ever since. Will you be free of the nightmares? No . . . they will just come less often," Aaron replied as he looked off into the distance to another time and another place.

"Ach, enough of these thoughts," he said as he stood up abruptly with his hand slicing through the air as if he were trying to push his own memories away.

"Here is the file with all the information you will need for your assignment in Washington. Now go. Study it. You will be leaving in two weeks. End of discussion."

David took the file and started for the door. He hesitated and then turned. "Thank you for everything, Aaron. I won't let you down. Sorry, I was such a whiner."

"Of course, you won't let us down. The Mossad knows what it is doing. What do you think we are anyway? School children?" Aaron smiled at his protégé as he left.

Once back at his desk, David opened the file and began to read. After an hour, he leaned back in his chair for a moment. "This might be an interesting assignment after all," he thought.

Connie O'Rourke, age 23. Father retired policeman from Boston Police Department, mother deceased, likes jazz, theater, and spy novels.

"Spy novels? You have got to be kidding. What is that all about?" he pondered. Subject is single and lives alone in an apartment in NW Washington, D.C. Dates occasionally, but prefers to socialize with friends from the C.I.A. She is highly intelligent and devoted to her boss at the C.I.A. Mossad feels the subject will be difficult to compromise.

"Difficult to compromise? How can that be? After all, aren't they sending the one person who has *charm*?" he whispered.

Your cover will be an American Agriculture student. "Unless absolutely necessary, always use things that you know for your cover in the field" were the words the instructors drummed into their heads. A split second of trying to remember a lie could cost you your life.

"Okay, being an agricultural student will be easy," he smiled. However, I am not comfortable with being an American though, David thought.

Americans have certain mannerisms that are unique and hard to copy. They seem to swagger and take up space unlike Europeans. Even from far away, you know they are Americans, because of the way they walk. My friend, Lev, thinks they're arrogant, but I don't agree with him. I think Americans act differently, because they are just so damn sure of themselves, David thought. Tomorrow I will ask Aaron if I can change my nationality to Swiss maybe. No good. Not much farming in the Alps. Maybe being Dutch or being from Belgium would work. He closed the file and locked it in his desk drawer.

Most of the people in his sector had gone home for the night. The cleaning crew had just entered to begin their work. David was lost in thought as he went to the elevator.

Two years ago, I certainly didn't think this would be my first assignment. Back then my rage was almost beyond control. All I wanted was revenge. The Mossad eventually caught the scum who slaughtered my family. Thank God. But, catching those animals and killing them wasn't enough. The rage is still with me just under the surface. I hate to admit this, but Aaron is right. I am still too emotional, but how the hell does one lose the memories and all those violent feelings? I have got to get myself under control. Exorcise this rage. Maybe getting out of Israel will help. Who knows? It could be worse. This Connie O'Rourke could have been horsey looking with buckteeth. And, deep down, admit it. You are anxious to see if you can *compromise* her – using charm, of course.

CHAPTER 2

TWO YEARS LATER – LANGLEY, VIRGINIA

"Hey, Sweetheart, bring us four coffees, will ya?"
Joe Aiello the head of the Code Desk asked as he
walked pass Connie's desk on his way to the meeting.

Connie flashed Joe an innocent smile. Ugh, men
can be so jerky sometimes. The name is Connie,
you idiot, she thought. Big deal, he didn't even
bother to look back at me to see my dazzling smile.
Ah well, it could be worse. I could be working for
"Hey Sweetheart" instead of Tom Bursak. She went
to get the coffee.

It really was a stroke of luck that Connie got the
job as Tom's secretary. He was the head of the entire

Russian desk here at Langley. Connie was assigned to Tom from the first day she started at the CIA.

"We don't normally start secretaries in a GS 9 position like this. You have to work your way up to that grade. But, since President Kennedy's assassination, things have become real tense with the Soviets. So, Tom Bursak has requested his secretary be fluent in Russian." the Personnel Director told her the day she started.

She remembered thinking, struggling through all those Russian language classes in college paid off. *Spaciba,* Professor Molinca for all the homework.

As Connie was getting the coffee, Sandy Lewinski from the European desk poked her head around the corner. Sandy was blond, cute and perky. She was the organizer for any and all parties in this Section. There wasn't a man on the floor – young, old, married or single, who didn't have erotic dreams of her. Although they all tried their best to get her into bed, none of them succeeded. Sandy was devoted and head-over-heels in love with her boyfriend, Sgt. Rick Loman who was serving in the Army in Vietnam. Despite her physical attributes, she had no pretensions. Connie liked her.

"You're still coming with us tonight, right Connie? We decided we're going to go into D.C. near the Naval Observatory. Staying around here in the Langley area is complete dullsville. I sure wish D.C. would stop with all those years of planning and just get that Metro built. Then, we could go where the action really is. Still . . . looking at guys in naval uniforms isn't too shabby either."

Connie smiled as she poured the cream into the creamer and set it on the tray. She stood with her hip against the counter. "Actually, thanks for picking the Naval Observatory area, it's near my apartment. What time and exactly where do I meet you?"

"Make that 7:30 at Farrell's on Wisconsin Avenue near Whitehaven Parkway."

"Oh, I know just where that is. I can walk there, because it's only about seven blocks from my apartment. Great. And, need I ask? Farrell's has been vetted, hasn't it? It's a place we're allowed to go?"

"Of course. I am Sandy the party planner. I checked with my friend in Surveillance. It has been checked out – no other spooks, except us frequent the place. See you tonight, kiddo."

Connie walked back to her office and stopped at her desk to put her note pad and a pencil on the coffee tray. She knocked on Tom's door before she entered. There were four men in Tom's office. Besides Tom and Joe Aiello, there was the head of the Eastern European desk, Jeff Evans, and Richard Morgan who worked under Jeff. Connie dubbed Richard, Mr. Gorgeous, because of his deep blue eyes.

Hopefully, the cup and saucer won't rattle when I hand the coffee to him, she thought.

After she was done – and not making a fool of herself with Mr. Gorgeous, she took her place in the remaining chair.

"Connie, you haven't missed anything. We haven't started this meeting yet," Tom said as he picked up the latest photos from Russia.

"Okay, guys, do we or do we not have updated information on the nuclear silos in the U.S.S.R. Last month's surveillance photos show increased building activities in Estonia near the Finish border, in East Germany, and in Bulgaria. These photos do not look like the Soviets are building more collective farms here," Tom said as he threw the photos back on his desk. "I want to know what the hell is going on. Joe, what have you got? Have you heard any noises about these sites?"

"Tom, so far, the communications we've picked up by the Soviets aren't saying a word about those three sites. And, they aren't transmitting with any new codes either."

"Shit," Tom blurted out. "Sorry Connie. I hope you didn't write that down."

Jeff took a sip of his coffee before he joined in the discussion. "Tom, I think we may have something for you. Although it's going to take some time to get it. Our agents are in the process of picking up a new Russian recruit. The guy works in the headquarters of the Soviet Army in Moscow. It was really strange. He approached the Danish Ambassador at an Embassy party asking him to pass along a note to the Americans. We don't know what to make of him yet. We're checking him out. His stepfather is Igor Polakova for crying out loud. So, we're going slowly, but he gave us troop movements in the Ukraine area that were legit."

Tom straightened in his chair. "Holy crap. Polakova is the second in command of the whole damn Soviet army. This could be a gold mine. What else have you got on this guy, Jeff?"

"His name is Nicholas Gregorovich. He is 26 years old and a graduate of the Soviet Military Academy.

He works for his stepfather. What we can't figure is why? He doesn't seem to want money. He hasn't made any mention of wanting to come over. Yet, he is willing to work for us. Right now we're working on the angle that he may be a double agent, because of Polakova. We don't have any photos of him yet either. But, his mother died yesterday."

Jeff turned in his chair. "Richard, can you arrange to have one of our agents get some photos of this guy at the funeral?"

"Of course. I'll send a cable to our Embassy as soon as the meeting is over, Jeff." Richard made a note on his pad.

"This sounds promising," Tom said. "Work as fast as you can, Jeff. Maybe this Gregorovich can help us out. NATO is on the DCI's back. Therefore, the DCI is on my back about these photos. We have got to know what the bastards are up to."

Connie took notes for the rest of the meeting. After the three men left, she waited for additional instructions from Tom.

"Listen, make the usual copies for this meeting. But, take out everything about this Gregorovich. Make one copy – eyes only. I don't know what the hell is going on here. But, this could really be big, so we might as well keep it quiet until we know more."

"Okay, Cupcake. Now tell me. What's the matter, Connie? You had a pinched look on your face during the meeting and it's still there. God, I would love to play poker with you. I'd win a bundle."

"Tom, I can't believe you're going to take pictures of this Russian at his own mother's funeral. That is so sick."

His look changed from amused to serious in a flash. He wasn't expecting her to say that. After working here for two years, maybe now was the time to get rid of that Pollyanna attitude of hers once and for all.

"No, it isn't sick, Connie. That's what we do. No emotion, no feeling, just get the job done any way we can. Just remember, whatever we are doing, our enemies are doing the same thing to us. Like it or not, that's our world."

"I love this job, Tom. And, I understand how important we are in the world. But, I just kept thinking of my mother's funeral and how horrible it would have been if there were people sneaking around with cameras."

"Ah, but when your mother died, you hadn't just approached the CIA with military secrets. Once Gregorovich did that, all bets were off. He now lives in a whole new world, kiddo, whether he knows it or not."

An hour later as Connie was finishing preparing the "Eyes Only" file, Richard Morgan approached her desk.

"I just want to thank you for getting the coffee for our meeting. I don't suppose it's a job you relish."

"Uh." Oh, great. Think of something to say, you idiot. She cleared her throat. "Thanks." Did I just squeak? Good grief, do you have a brain in your head? It's those blue eyes of his. They're driving me nuts!

Richard lifted one eyebrow and smiled at Connie. "I'm almost afraid to ask this, because it could turn into a long night with only one word answers, but, would you like to have dinner with me? I thought we could go into Georgetown."

She straightened her shoulders and said, "I am capable of two and even three word answers. And, yes I would like to have dinner with you."

"I am going to be out of town this weekend – hush, hush business you know," he said as he imitated Groucho Marx with an imaginary cigar. "But, are you free next Friday?"

"Yes, I'm free. How's that? Have I dazzled you with my extensive vocabulary?"

"You have. I'll stop by next week as to the time, okay? Just shake your head if yes. I don't want to put more strain on your vocal chords." Richard said as he gave Connie the most fantastic smile and walked away.

Oh, Mr. Gorgeous you have made my day. No. You, handsome hunk, you have made my year.

CHAPTER 3

TWO YEARS LATER – MOSCOW CEMETERY

Nicholas threw the rose on his mother's coffin as it was being lowered into the grave. He was numb as he watched the coffin descend. Ah, dear Mother, how I loved you, he thought.

Once the coffin reached the bottom, the cemetery workers removed the straps. Now each mourner would throw a shovel of dirt into the grave until the hole was filled. As her son, it was his duty to begin the ritual. He picked up the shovel lying on the mound of dirt. Stepping on the rim, he pushed it deep into the dirt. He knew when he was done he would have to hand the shovel to his stepfather. It would be the hardest thing he ever had to do.

Only once did he glance at Igor while he stood at his mother's grave. There were no tears in Igor's eyes. Good, he thought. If you even tried to put on a show of sorrow, I would drive a stake right through your heart, right here, right now.

As he handed the shovel to Igor, he looked at him again. The intense loathing must have shown on his face, because he heard Igor take in a breath of air as he blinked and jerked backwards in surprise.

Careful, careful Nicholas thought as he softened his features and stepped back.

Once the grave was filled in, the mourners walked to the outer gates of the cemetery for the traditional shots of vodka. This was the Russians' way of saying their final goodbye to the dead.

Nicholas was just about to take a glass from the tray when Ivan Petrovich from the Military Archives came up to him and gave him a bear hug.

"Ah, Ivan, I saw you standing at the grave. Thank you for coming," he said as he hugged him back and held the hands of the old man.

"Your mother is with your father now, Nicholas. She was a saint. She is with God now too. I know we are no longer supposed to say that. But, the government cannot take away our memories. I remember the Church. It is still in my heart," Ivan said as he swiped away a tear with sleeve of his coat.

Thank goodness they were standing apart from the other mourners. Hopefully, no one heard Ivan, groaned Nicholas silently. "My friend," he said as he leaned closer to the old man and spoke softly in his ear. "I understand, but you must keep those thoughts to yourself."

Nicholas loved his beloved country of Russia. But, he was no fool. Sometimes it seemed that the Russian people had merely changed yokes – from the yoke of the Czars to the yoke of Communism. Of course, just like Ivan, Nicholas had to keep those thoughts buried deep within him. If he wanted to continue to rise in the Soviet military, he knew voicing any thoughts of criticism would end his career in a flash. But, sometimes late at night after drinking vodka, the longing for a better Russia would overwhelm him. Oh, come now, he would think at those times. Vodka automatically makes everyone weep for something better. If this were the Garden of Eden, give a Russian a bottle of vodka, and he would find something wrong with that place too.

After Nicholas had the obligatory shots of vodka with the rest of the mourners, he got in his car and drove to his mother's house. He needed to be surrounded by his past.

No one paid any attention to the lone man who had been standing beside another grave in the cemetery. As the mourners departed, the man walked out through the gate at the opposite end.

What would life be like if my father had lived, Nicholas thought as he stood in the living area of his mother's house and looked around. There would have been laughter. He knew that. It was the one thing that had been missing for many years. He went into his mother's bedroom and sat down in her favorite chair by the window. The vodka was taking its toll. Soon he fell asleep.

It was dark outside when he awoke. For a moment Nicholas was confused trying to remember where he was. When he realized he was in his mother's chair, overwhelming grief took him by surprise. He began sobbing uncontrollably. Slowly, he got himself under control. He blew his nose and wiped away his tears with his handkerchief. He tried to keep his thoughts on his mother, but memories of Igor kept intruding.

"I have got to get him out of my mind," yelled Nicholas shattering the stillness of the house.

This cannot go on, he thought wildly. I will get my revenge and then be done with Igor forever. But, the Americans are dragging their feet. They haven't contacted me in three weeks. I have more to give you, you stupid idiots. His contact actually told him the Americans thought he was a double agent sent by his stepfather. What a joke. Igor ruined the life of my parents and now he is ruining my revenge. I can't let that happen.

This insanity of mine can destroy everything. I almost blew it at the cemetery this morning. I need to plan this revenge carefully. It must look like Igor is the one who is leaking military secrets to the Americans. He is the one who must be destroyed. If I keep on in this reckless fashion, everything will point to me as the traitor. The son of a bitch will end up winning once more.

Nicholas spent that night and the morning of the next day making his plans. He was ready for the Americans. Now if they would only make contact.

CHAPTER 4

Sandy Lewinski came off the dance floor smiling and chatting with her latest dance partner. The sailor from the Naval Observatory escorted her back to the table where the group from the CIA was sitting.

The young sailor said, "Thanks, Sandy. Boy, you Department of Justice people sure know how to dance." Sandy flashed him a smile and watched him walk away.

"So, that's who you are tonight? You work for the DOJ? And, just what do you do, Counselor?" Connie asked laughing.

"Oh, you know as well as I do, the minute we tell people we work for the CIA, they start pestering us for secrets. It's just easier not to mention it at all," Sandy said.

"You know, Sandy, I can never figure you out. How you can be so in love with your cutie pie, Rick. Yet, you have been dancing with every sailor in the place," Connie said as she watched her friend scope out another sailor.

"Oh, Rick and I have an understanding. Before he left for Nam, we decided each of us can look and have fun, but what we do never betrays our commitment to each other. Dancing doesn't do any harm. And, just look at all these guys. Aren't they beautiful? I just love looking at their butts. I can't stand guys that have little skinny behinds. I like wide ones like Rick's. They turn me on. What do you look at when you look at guys, Connie?"

"I look at a guy's mouth. The lips have to curve in a certain way. It's hard to explain. But, I can imagine all sorts of dreamy things just by looking at his mouth. I can't stand mushy full lips. That turns me off."

"Well, isn't that exciting. It may explain why you have been sitting here all night *thinking* about dancing. By the way, who are you going to be tonight? How about you work for the Secret Service?" Sandy asked enthusiastically.

Connie shook her head. "I've decided to be someone dull and boring. I am going to say I work for the Department of Commerce. How's that for Miss Excitement? Kind of goes right along with looking at guys' mouths, don't you think?" Connie replied as another young man came to ask Sandy to dance.

As Sandy was getting up, she leaned over and said, "Don't be too boring, Connie, or you'll miss all the fun."

As Connie watched her friend walk to the dance floor, she debated whether to tell Sandy about her hot date with Richard Morgan next Friday. If I tell her I won't seem so dull and boring. But, if I tell her, it will be all over the office Monday morning. I would hate that. I'm too private a person to have people gossiping about me. I'll just sit here and look bland.

When the dance was over, Sandy had her dance partner by the hand and was leading him back to their table. She gave Connie a wink as she introduced him.

"Connie, this is David. David this is Connie. Isn't he cute? Come on, David, pull up a chair and sit down. Don't be dull," Sandy whispered in Connie's ear as he retrieved a vacant chair from the next table. David Levi sat down between Sandy and Connie.

"Hello," he said as he gave Connie a shy smile.

Good heavens, he really is cute thought Connie.

He shook her hand and said, "I am David Zeigler. Do you work with Sandy?"

"No, I work for the Department of Commerce."

Sandy rolled her eyes and made an imaginary square in the air. Sandy was right. I should have picked something more exciting. This guy has the most interesting brown eyes. And, that mouth! Oh, boy, I wonder if he's a good kisser?

"I am from Holland. Everything is new to me here in this country. What is the Department of Commerce and what do you do there?"

"I count trucks." Connie said. She heard Sandy groan and lower her head. "What are you doing here in the States? Are you working?"

"No, I am a university student working on my Master's degree in Agriculture. I am attending Georgetown."

Whoa! Ding, ding, ding – alarm bells, Connie thought. What is going on here? Georgetown doesn't have a School of Agriculture. I doubt any of those Hoya's would know a rose bush from a potato plant. Just my luck, this hunk is probably a used car salesman from Milwaukee. But, he has an unusual accent. I just can't place it. Well, let's play this out for a while and see where it goes.

"How interesting. What is your area of emphasis?" If he says tulips, for sure he sells cars.

"My emphasis is irrigation. Holland has an abundance of dikes and windmills. It is a very low-lying country that can flood easily. So, my country is interested in testing worldwide crops that may be conducive to a wet and colder climate."

All right. Score one for the Flying Dutchman. But something is wrong with that accent. I'll bet my wooden shoes this guy is not Dutch. Connie's thoughts were interrupted when Sandy stood up preparing to leave. Everyone at the table started to laugh when Sandy announced she had to leave, because she was trying a big case in court tomorrow.

Smiling, Connie checked the time on her wristwatch. "Oh, it is getting late. I think it's time for me to leave too.

"Well, it was nice to meet you, David," she said as she extended her hand to him. "Good luck with your studies at, ah, Georgetown."

After the handshake, David helped her with her coat. "Can I see you home?" he asked.

Let's see there is Sandy who is cute as can be. Then there's me – Miss Department of Commerce lady. He wants to see me home? What is going on here?

"Oh, that's okay, David," Connie answered. "Don't bother. I'll be fine. Besides, I only live seven blocks from here; and, I'm walking."

"In my country, men don't let ladies walk alone at night. It is too dangerous. I'll walk you to your door," David said as he gave her a smile.

More alarm bells went off. Since when is *Holland* too dangerous? What? Are those nasty Belgians coming across the border causing havoc again? Well, this is going to be one of the dumbest things I have ever done, but . . .

"All right. You can catch a cab one block away from my apartment," she smiled right back at him. I've got news for you, Bubb. You will be walking me to the door not through the door.

Connie caught a glimpse of Sandy grinning and giving her the okay sign. She just raised an eyebrow at Sandy as she passed her.

Once out on the sidewalk, they began to talk. In a short time, they reached Connie's apartment building.

Good grief. How did we get here so quickly? This was very nice. David is easy to talk with, Connie thought.

"Well, here we are," she said as she opened the door of the apartment lobby. "If you go down that block to the corner, you should be able to hail a cab. It's a main street and there are cabs going up and down all night."

Oh, nuts. I don't want the evening to end. Do I, or don't I invite him up for a cup of coffee? Is he going to think I want to go to bed with him just because I'm offering coffee? I hate awkward moments like this.

"Look, Connie. I am just going to be forward here. I've enjoyed talking with you. I would like to continue. Can you invite me up for a cup of coffee?" David said looking hopeful.

"I am enjoying myself too, David. You're in luck. Not only do I have coffee, I have chocolate chip cookies too. Ah, just so you ah know . . .it's coffee that I am offering."

"If you'll notice, it was only coffee I asked for," David smiled.

Connie's apartment was on the fourth floor of the building. The front door opened directly into

31

the living room. The sofa and chairs were stuffed and comfortable looking. Seating was arranged to take in the view through the sliding patio doors on the opposite wall. The colors were quiet greens, muted yellows, browns and tans. There was no chrome or metal in sight. At the right of the entry-way stood a wood, floor to ceiling bookcase that held books, mementos, and pictures.

David took off his coat and laid it over one of the stuffed chairs. He walked over to the bookcase as Connie went into the kitchen to prepare the coffee. Most of the books on the shelves were spy novels.

"Why do you have so many spy novels, Connie?"

"Oh, that is my one weakness," she laughed as she peeked around the corner. "I have been reading mystery and spy novels since I was in grade school. I don't know if you have Nancy Drew Mysteries in Holland, but I have every one in the collection. I started with those in fifth grade and have gone nuts ever since. Once in a while, I try to read one of the classics so I don't appear to be a total idiot."

"Do you mind if I smoke?" David asked while he looked around for an ashtray.

Connie came to the doorway of her kitchen. "I don't mind. But, can you smoke out on the patio?

I don't like the smell of smoke in my apartment. There's an ashtray on the table out there." David crossed the room, opened the door and stepped out into the cool night air.

He lit his cigarette and stood at the railing as he looked out at the lights of the city.

Beautiful, he thought. I don't know what it is, but there is something magical about looking at big cities at night. From up here, the city is so quite and the lights outlining the buildings are very calming. Tel Aviv was the same for me. For my first assignment, I did not expect to be feeling like this – not only this magnificent view, but Connie herself.

When we were in the bar, I thought the assignment was going to be so easy. Why the hell did the Mossad think she was intelligent? She sounded like a complete fool saying she counted trucks. It was going to be a snap. She probably wouldn't even realize she would be giving me the information I needed. He was relieved – at least she was good looking. The dark auburn hair and green eyes were very enticing.

But, on the walk home, things changed dramatically. We talked like two old friends. There is nothing phony about her. Everything is there on her face. She is warm, funny, kind, and definitely not stupid. It's like I have known her all my life. And, it all happened in just seven blocks. Another time, another place and I would be trying to spend as much time as I could with her. He let out a short breath of air, get a grip, Mr. Charming Master Spy. Israel needs that information. He turned as he heard the patio door slide open.

"Would you like to have coffee out here?" Connie asked as she joined him at the railing. "You know, I just love looking at the city at night. It seems so peaceful. I know there are probably terrible things happening on the streets down there, but up here, in the quiet, it's a different world." Connie smiled.

Both remained quiet as they looked at the city. "Well," breaking the spell of the moment, "I'll get the coffee."

She brought it out and they sat down at the small table.

"Tell me, David, what do you read? Are you hooked on spy novels too?"

"I'm not much of a reader. I have been so busy with school that I haven't had much free time."

Hmmm. Definitely, doesn't sound like Dutch to me. He had trouble pronouncing *th* in the words *with* and *that*. They came out as *wis* and *zat*.

He should have said *vis* not *wis*. And, the *ar* was not right when he said free? There is some Slavic in your background, kiddo. Where have I heard that accent before? It was just recently too.

David saw Connie look at him oddly. In order to change the subject, he said, "Your father is a policeman, isn't he?"

"Yes, he was," she said frowning. "How did you know?"

Oh, great – why don't you just tell her you know that because it's in her dossier at the Mosad. "Well, I, ah, just assumed the picture in the bookcase of the man in the uniform was your father," he said.

"Yup. That's my Dad," Connie smiled. "He was a policeman in the Boston Police Department. What does your father do?"

Connie was shocked as she watched David's face drain of color. I just hurt him, she thought. What did I do? It was a normal question.

"My father died a few years ago," David said quietly as he took in a deep breathe of air. "I'm sorry. I did not expect that question. I was quite close to my father. I still miss him." He stood up.

"It's getting late. I'd better be going. Thanks for the coffee, Connie," David said as he walked back into her apartment and retrieved his coat.

Whatever happened, I sure hurt him by asking about his father. This is such an awkward moment. I feel so bad about this.

"Ah, thank you too, David, for the nice evening. I'm glad I met you," she said as she walked him to the door.

When he walked out the door into the hall, he turned to face her. "I would like to see you again," he said with a frown on his face. "I, um, I'm trying to decide whether to kiss you good night or not," he blurted out. "Oh, Hell. I am going to kiss you. I have been thinking about doing it all night." He leaned forward and took her in his arms.

Connie smiled at him as she put her arms around his shoulders. "Oh, good. Those lips of yours have been driving me crazy all evening too," she chuckled. "Kiss me. You fool," she said laughingly.

Whoa! Oh, my gosh, Connie thought as she grabbed the collar of David's jacket and deepened the kiss trying to get more of him. What the heck is happening? I didn't expect such a reaction. I did not expect the fireworks.

David's arms circled tighter around her waist. He responded as urgently as she did. His hand slid up to her breast.

Oops–too fast, Connie thought breathlessly as she pulled back and put her hands flat on David's shoulders. "Oh, wow, I did not expect that. What is going on between us, David?" she said looking up at him.

"Oy," David said softly as he put his head on her forehead and stood with his arms still around her waist.

Oy? Oy? Jewish! That's it! He's Israeli! His accent is just like the Israelis who have been on the news being interviewed about the Six Days War. That's where I heard that accent! An Israeli who says he is Dutch and a student at Georgetown studying for a degree they don't even offer. Why? Oh, Ho! You little devil. Only one answer. You have got to be from the Mossad. I'll be darned.

Connie stepped back from David as she gently pushed him back out into the hall. She looked directly in his eyes, wiggled her eyebrows and smiled. "I wouldn't mind kissing you again. But, just to be clear. I have no intention of ever telling you anything about the Department of Commerce . . . Boychick." She winked as she closed the door in his face.

"What the hell just happened?" David whispered at the closed door.

CHAPTER 5

David was dumbfounded as he walked to the elevator. Calling him "Boychick" was like a kick in the teeth. How the hell did Connie know he was Jewish? And, then that cryptic message about not saying anything about the Department of Commerce, how did she figure out Mossad?

"Now what am I going to do?" he whispered as he pushed the down button. Great. I failed on my first assignment. Jerk. When the elevator door opened, David did not get in. He just stood there staring into the elevator. He remained where he was as the door slide closed.

"Well, I blew it. I can go home in absolute shame. Or, I can salvage some of my dignity and learn from this," he mumbled. He turned around, went back to Connie's apartment and rang the doorbell.

When she opened the door there was a twinkle in her eyes and a smile on her face.

"How did you know?" he simply said.

"Oy".

"Oy? That's it?"

"Yeah, when you said 'Oy' after you kissed me, and very brilliantly I might add, I knew you were Jewish. And, then everything else fell into place – the fake Dutch accent, the nonsense about getting your Agricultural degree at Georgetown, the comment about the streets of Holland being so dangerous at night."

"Good grief, Connie. Was I really that obvious? Didn't I do anything right?"

"I'm sorry. I didn't mean to deflate your ego. Honest. Come on back in. Let's talk." She took David's hand and led him back into her apartment.

"I have a question for you. Why me? Why on earth is the Mossad interested in me?" she asked.

He took off his coat and sat down on the sofa next to her. For a quiet moment, they looked out her patio doors at the night skyline. He debated about what to tell her. Everything in his training demanded he keep silent. But, the naivety of youth took over.

He turned to her and said, "It was the Six Days War. We need help. We need answers about who is pulling the strings in the Middle East. We can't be caught like that again."

"And, they sent you here to me with those questions? David, I don't know anything about the Middle East."

"No, but you have access to what the Russians are up to in the Middle East. The Mossad felt since you worked for Tom Bursak, you would know those things."

"What? Are you kidding? The Mossad knows that I work at the CIA? They even know the name of my boss? They have a file on me!"

Instead of being frightened by the fact she was known to the Mossad, Connie put her hands on either side of David's face and gave him a big kiss. She began to laugh as she pulled away.

"Hold on a second I have to get something." Connie jumped up and ran to the bottom drawers of her bookcase. She fell to her knees and frantically began opening and closing the drawers.

"Where is it? Rats. I know I put it in here somewhere," she fumed as she pushed things aside.

"What are you doing? What is it you're looking for, Connie?" David asked bewildered.

"Aha! I knew it. I knew I stashed it in here," she smiled as she pulled out the battered, black fedora. She put the hat on and turned to look at David. "What do you think? Do I look like a real spy?" Connie said as she rakishly pulled the brim over one eye and returned to the sofa.

Connie couldn't stop beaming as she proceeded to tell David the story behind the hat. "So you see, David, you have given me the opportunity to come as close to the world of intrigue as I'll ever get." She threw her arms around him. "Oh, I can't tell you how happy I am. Now, tell me the rest." And, he did.

"So you're saying we aren't helping you? I find that so hard to believe. David, this is a mess. I can't tell you what I know about the Russians. You know that. Oh, these games we play can get so stupid and frustrating. And, I also have to let my boss know you approached me. I'm sorry, David, but I have to do that."

"I know. I don't blame you. I'd do the same thing."

They were quiet again as they sat beside one another. Each knew they were walking a very fine line. Both worked in a world of distrust and secrets. Finally, Connie raised one eyebrow and asked, "How long are you going to be in Washington?"

David shook his head and snorted. "Originally, until I compromised you. Now, I'll probably see if I can get a flight out tomorrow. No use prolonging the inevitable of admitting I blew it."

"No. Wait a few days. Let me see what I can do. I want to talk to my boss about this."

"What are you planning on telling him? That you were approached by the most inept agent on the planet?"

Connie chuckled. "Don't be so hard on yourself, David. How can someone be inept when he is such a good kisser?" she chuckled. "Listen, I am going to tell Tom exactly what you told me and see if he can help. So, don't leave until I find out what he has to say."

David looked doubtful. "Mmm, Connie I don't think . . ."

"Look, it can't hurt to try. I have to report this anyway. By the way, your real name is David, isn't it?"

"Yeah, it's David. But the last name is not Zeigler."

"And . . . finish it. I don't think it will make much difference at this point if you tell me your real name."

"David Levi. Actually, David Karoly Levi."

"Ah, Karoly. You've got some Hungarian in you, haven't you."

David looked startled. "You are amazing me more and more. Yes, I do. It was my mother who was Hungarian."

"You said *was*. Your mother *was* Hungarian. When I asked you about your father, your face showed so much pain," Connie said softly. "David, what happened to your parents? I know I hurt you very deeply when I asked about your father. I never meant to do that. I am so sorry."

He looked at her in puzzlement? Why is this stranger so easy to talk to? What is it about her? She can zero right in to the heart of things.

"I'm a Jew. My boss said because of that most of us have to carry around our past. My mother and father and my sister were killed," he began slowly.

As David continued, Connie started to cry silently. She put one arm around David's shoulder and took his hand in hers as the tears streamed down her face. They continued to sit there without moving long after David had finished speaking.

"Tomorrow I am going to do everything I can to help you, David. You are not inept. You are the most outstanding and courageous person I have ever met," Connie said quietly.

CHAPTER 6

The Russian man in the tattered clothing and worn, leather hat approached the house on the outskirts of Moscow. He was carrying a tool kit. Instead of entering by the front door, he walked around to the side of the house, as any tradesman would be expected to do and knocked on the back door.

"Da?" Nicholas asked as he answered the door.

"I am here to fix your plumbing problem, Comrade," the workman said in fluent Russian. He then lowered his voice and said softly, "Invite me in. I am your new handler for the Americans."

"You know where I live?" Nicholas was appalled.

"Keep your voice down, Comrade. And, open the damn door," hissed the American agent.

What a pain in the ass these new recruits were, he thought. They have no concept of how to act or the danger they put themselves and their handlers in with their screw-ups. With the houses so close, any of his neighbors would have been able to hear him. This guy has a lot to learn if he wants to keep on living.

"Yes, my plumbing. Of course," Nicholas said as he stepped back from the open door.

Nicholas' handler was the top CIA field agent here in Moscow. With the stakes as high as something involving Igor Polakova's stepson, the CIA had to send its best. He walked across the kitchen and pulled the curtains closed on the window over the sink. Without saying another word, the Handler proceeded to go from room to room checking for any evidence of listening devices.

When he was through with his inspection, he saw the frantic look on Nicholas' face.

Oh, geez. Here we go. The new recruit is hitting the panic button. These guys all think everything is going to be so easy. Just hand over the documents and go merrily along living the same, normal life. There will be no change in their lives whatsoever. Well, Buddy, I've got news for you. By contacting us, you just entered the *Twilight Zone* and nothing in your life will ever be the same again. If you think you are going to walk away before we even get started, think again, asshole, because we've got you now. Time to calm him down.

"Comrade, come sit down. Let's talk for a while," the Handler, who had been through this before, said calmly. He smiled and looked Nicholas in the eyes as he sat down and motioned to the other chair at the kitchen table. He looked around and said, "This is a nice house. You grew up here, right?" Get them to talk about the things they know and feel comfortable with.

"Yes, I did grow up here. This was my mother's house and now it is mine." Nicholas began slowly. He looked down at his hands and then looked up at the Handler. "You are Russian. Are you not? How did the Americans recruit you?"

The minute Nicholas said the word "recruit", the Handler could see the panic return to his eyes. Here it comes, he thought.

"Listen, I'm not ready. I must think about this," Nicholas said as he rose and began pacing the room. The Handler remained calm as he watched his contact.

"Nicholas, I want you to sit back down and stay sitting while we talk." He pushed the chair out with his foot as he said this. "I am not here to ask for anything from you. We will talk. That's all for now. You asked if I was Russian. I am, but I wasn't born here. I was born in the United States after my parents emigrated there. Now, tell me about yourself."

Nicholas gave a raw laugh as he looked as his Handler. "If you know where I live and when I would be home then you know all about me. There is nothing to add. Look in your files if you want more."

"Good one, Comrade," the Handler said as he smiled. He is showing some backbone.

Nicholas sat looking over the Handler. "Why, would the Americans send such a slovenly looking man as you?"

The Handler raised his eyebrows and nodded his head at Nicholas. "Looks can be deceiving. How else could I contact you at your home, unless I was dressed as a tradesman. What would your neighbors think if I came here in a suit? There would be too much gossip, Comrade."

"I see. Very good," Nicholas responded. "So what do we do now? What is the procedure for what I am doing?"

"Going back to your earlier statement about having files that know all about you. We do know many things about you, Nicholas. But, here are some things we don't know. We don't know what it is you want from us? And, more importantly, we don't know why you decided to contact us? What set you off?" he said looking deep into Nicholas' eyes? "We need to know these things before we can move forward."

Nicholas stared at the Handler as he sat with his elbows on his knees and his hands clasped. He said nothing as he got up and went to the cupboard. He retrieved a bottle of vodka and two glasses and brought them back to the table. He poured the clear liquid into the glasses and handed one to the American. After Nicholas downed his drink, he breathed in deeply and looked at the Handler still remaining silent. It was very quiet in the room as they sat there. They could hear children playing in the street and birds chirping in the trees. So normal.

"My step father, Igor Polakova, had my father killed during the War," he began. "I found a document in his handwriting laying out the plans for my father's death." Nicholas refilled the glasses with more vodka.

Here is where I have to be careful thought the Handler. The Russian motto known from childhood on is *an open bottle is an empty bottle.* I am not going back to write my report only to reel up the steps of the Embassy in a drunken stupor. He left his glass untouched.

"What I want is the destruction of my step father. I want what I do and what I provide to you to point to Igor. I want you to help me ruin him," Nicholas said angrily. "You know, I don't think of myself as the traitor in this scenario. I love my country. The Russian people are good people. I don't think of this as destroying my country. I think of this as destroying Igor. Will you help me?"

I'll be damned thought the Handler. This is a gold mine that has fallen into our laps. This whole thing has just reached monumental proportions. We might be able to bring down the second in command of the whole Soviet Army. We need to go slowly and do it right.

"We can help you, Nicholas. We will meet again to talk further. But, now I need to think about the best way to get that revenge for you."

If we do this right, it will strike a huge hole in the Soviet military. It is important now to make him think we are working with him. We are on his side. Make him think this is about him; because chances are by the time this is over, Nicholas will be dead.

"We will meet again in one week. I will come here to your house Sunday afternoon with a plan to help you get your revenge."

"Here, take this piece of chalk," the Handler said as he pulled it from his pocket. "From now on, if you ever have to contact me, go to Gorky Park. Enter the Park through the Lenin Street entrance and leave a chalk mark on the right side of the first pillar of the fence along the river. Just make a simple, short line on the pillar like this," he said as he drew a line on the table and then handed the chalk to Nicholas. I will contact you as soon as it is safe to do so, when I see that line.

Nicholas looked at the Handler. "What is your name? If my life is in your hands, I would at least like to know your name."

"Ivan. My name is Ivan."

"That's not your real name, is it?"

"No, it is not," the Handler replied softly. He wouldn't explain, let him figure out. If Nicholas was ever caught and tortured, he wouldn't be able to name his contact. Poor bastard.

CHAPTER 7

Connie straightened the stapler for the tenth time along with everything else on her desk while she thought about the best way to tell Tom the Mossad approached her last night. What I hate about this whole thing is that I am going to have to tell Tom and then go through the vetting process with Internal Security. What a pain that will be, because nothing really happened. This will be blown out of proportion. It was bad enough dealing with Sandy Lewinski this morning when she cornered me in the copy room.

"So . . .what happened? Are you going to see David again? What did you two talk about? Did he kiss you? He was so cute. You two would make a perfect couple," Sandy bubbled over.

"Hey, one question at a time, Sandy," Connie laughed. "David just walked me to my apartment and then caught a cab after that. Nothing happened and I doubt I'll be seeing him again," Connie lied. I hate lying. I hope I am carrying this off.

"That's it? Oh, Connie, how sad. He was so adorable. I had such high hopes for you." Sandy looked at her with such sad eyes.

Connie retrieved the copies from the machine and walked back to her desk. Sandy, if I could only tell you what really happened last night. You would have a whole new image of me.

Just as she was about to leave her desk to talk to Tom, Richard Morgan approached carrying an envelope.

"Morning, Connie," Richard said with a smile. "Is Tom available? By the way, can I pick you up around 7:00 pm this Friday for our dinner?"

"I'll see if Tom can see you now," she said as she dialed his extension. While waiting, she wrote her address and phone number on a note pad.

"Tom, Richard Morgan is here to see you."

"Okay, I'll send him in."

Connie finished writing, tore the page out of her pad and handed it to Richard. "Here is my address and phone number. See you Friday at seven," she said as she paused staring at him.

"Oh, ah, and, you can go right in. Tom is waiting for you." Ugh. *This is worse than when I was a teenager.*

Richard entered Tom's office and closed the door behind him. As he walked to Tom's desk, he said, "Here are the photos of the new Russian recruit, Nicholas Gregorovich, Tom." Without being asked, he proceeded to sit in the chair in front of Tom's desk. He leaned back and crossed his ankle over his knee.

"As you can see, we got some good shots of the guy at his mother's funeral along with some of the other people who were also there."

Tom opened the envelope and studied the photos. "They are good. What does your boss think about them?"

"I haven't showed them to Jeff yet. I brought them directly to you first. I know how important you think this guy is."

Tom became very still. He did not move his head but merely moved his eyes from the photos up to Richard and said, "How did you know Gregorovich was important to me?"

Richard was thrown off balance. And, he did not like the look in Tom's eyes. He wasn't about to tell Tom he knew the Russian was important, because he spotted the "eyes only" file for Gregorovich on Connie's desk last week.

"Well, you seemed excited about him during our meeting last week." he said as he uncrossed his leg and sat straighter in his chair. "I just thought you would like to see them as soon as they came in."

"All right," Tom responded. "Thanks. You can go now." As Richard started to rise, Tom added, "A piece of advice, Richard. There is a chain of command here at the CIA. Your boss should always be the first to know. Never skip a level with information."

Richard couldn't believe Tom could possibly say something like that to him. He kept his composure, but was seething inside. One day I am going to have your job, you Slavic peasant, he thought as he looked at Tom.

"My mistake, Tom," he said unctuously. "I will go to Jeff from now on."

Tom continued to stare at the door after Richard left. Something is going on with that guy. What's his agenda? He needs to be watched, he thought.

After a moment, he rang for Connie to give her the photos to be filed.

"Well, one inquisition over, on to the next," Connie mumbled as she started toward Tom's office. Okay, the best way will be just tell Tom everything and see what happens. I have no intention of lying to him like I did to Sandy, she thought as she entered his office.

"Tom, I need to speak with you. Do you have a minute?" Connie said as she sat down in the chair Richard had vacated moments ago.

"I'm glad you're here, Connie. I want you to file these photos of Nicholas Gregorovich in the "eyes-only" file. Now what's up, kiddo? You look worried."

"Tom," Connie started then stopped.

"Tom, last night I was approached by the Mossad.

"What!"

"But, nothing happened. Well, something did happen, but not what you think happened. Okay, I kissed him, but that was before I knew he was Mossad. Then he said, 'Oy.' And, then everything fell into place; and I knew David was from the Mossad."

"Connie."

"I didn't say anything, Tom. It was all so innocent. Sandy danced with him and brought him back to the table and then he walked me home and came up for a cup of coffee."

"Connie, stop."

"And, now I am going to be vetted and this will be blown out of proportion, when all David wanted to know was what are the Russians up to in the Middle East. He told me that. I didn't tell him that. What I told him was that I wouldn't tell him anything about the Department of Commerce.

"The Department of What?"

And, then this morning I lied to Sandy. I hate lying. Oh, no. Now I am going to start crying. I laid awake all night, Tom, thinking about this and how I was going to tell you. And, I am telling…"

"STOP!"

"Stop right there, Connie," Tom said as he handed her the handkerchief from his pocket. "Let's take this slowly and from the beginning. Don't leave anything out. How and where did you meet this guy? How did you know he was from the Mossad? What did he ask you to do? And, how did you respond?"

Connie took a deep breath to calm herself; and, then she began at the beginning from when she met David at Farrell's, the information the Mossad wanted, what happened to his parents, right up to the time she said good night to him.

As Tom sat listening to her, he became angry and stunned the Mossad would even approach his secretary. He was also amused and proud as he realized Connie pegged the agent right from the start. His mind was racing as he sorted though everything she was telling him.

By remaining quiet as Connie spoke, Tom allowed her to get her thoughts in order and tell him everything. Connie felt the weight of the world had left her shoulders when she finished speaking. She was able to think rationally and calmly now that he knew what happened to her.

"Tom, why can't we tell the Israelis what the Russians are doing in the Middle East? I don't understand that. David was right when he said they are alone in this. Can't we help them?"

"Connie, it's not that simple. It's not just the CIA. There are other areas of the government that are involved in this. What we do, the world doesn't know about. What the President and the State Department do goes on the national news every night.

"Listen, kiddo, you have dropped a bomb here. I need time to organize my thoughts as to the best way to handle what happened to you. I'm going to talk to some people. But, right now, I am furious the Mossad had the gall to contact you, Connie. Those S.O.B.s had no right to get my secretary involved in this at all. That will be the first issue I am going to take of," Tom fumed.

"I don't want to be vetted, Tom," Connie said quietly. "I never said a word. If Internal Security comes in, I will be treated like a leper for the rest of my life. I swear to you, nothing happened last night."

"I thought you said something did happen. Don't I recall you mentioning something about a big, sloppy kiss?" Tom smiled as he tried to lighten the mood.

"Yeah, well, just so you know, it wasn't sloppy. It was pretty darn good though," Connie laughed.

"Okay, Connie, let me see what I can do without getting you involved. Again, I need time to sort through all of this. Now go back to your desk. Understand – this isn't the end of the world. Geez, you really got yourself right in the middle of espionage, didn't you?" Tom chuckled. "You always said you wanted to be a spy. Well, kiddo, how does it feel? Not like all those novels you read, is it?" he said turning serious.

"No. Reading a novel curled up on the couch under a blanket isn't the same as the real deal. Thanks, Tom. I feel better having talked to you."

"Oh, by the way, I almost forgot. Give me that envelop of photos back," he said reaching across his desk. "And, call Jeff Evans. Tell him I want to see him today.

CHAPTER 8

An hour later, Tom came out of his office. He stopped at Connie's desk. "I'm going to lunch and will be out of the office for about two hours, if anyone needs me." He gave Connie a quick wink and a smile as he walked away. She still looked rattled about their discussion earlier this morning.

Don't worry kid. I am going to make sure something like this doesn't happen to you again, Tom thought as he pushed the button to the elevator. When it arrived he got in and took it down to the garage. Once in his car, he drove out of Langley and turned south.

"Before, I do anything else, I am going to make one phone call to make sure the Mossad never tries this again," Tom muttered. But, in order to make the call, he needed to use a phone that wasn't bugged. He couldn't do it from his office.

"If I call from my office, not only will the CIA know who I am calling, but the entire conversation will be recorded. They will know it was Connie who was approached," he said quietly as he headed for Pimmit Hills, Virginia.

Twenty-five minutes later after he made a series of turns to make sure he wasn't being followed, Tom pulled into a Shell gas station. It had a phone booth on the side of the station away from the pumps. He parked his car and grabbed the roll of quarters she kept in the glove compartment of his car. He hoped the overseas call wouldn't require more than his one roll of quarters. He checked for any unusual activity in the area as he walked to the phone. There was none.

"Why should there be? No one has a clue about this yet," he decided as he inserted the quarters and dialed the International phone number.

On the third ring far away in Israel, Aaron Zucker answered his phone, "Shalom?"

"You son of a bitch, Aaron. What the hell do you think you're doing involving my secretary in your Mossad plots?" Tom roared from six thousand miles away.

"Ah, Mr. Bursak. And, how is the weather in D.C.?" Aaron said calmly. "Whatever are you talking about, My Boy?"

"Don't hand me that 'My Boy' crap. You know exactly what I am talking about. How dare you even think about sending an agent to involve Connie? She's just a kid, for crying out loud. You crossed the line on this one, Aaron. And, you know it. There are certain people that are off limits. If you ever try something this underhanded again, I swear I will make sure no agency in the world gives you anything ever again – not even the correct time," Tom threatened. "And, you know I can do it too, Aaron."

"Tom, my old friend. You know as well as I do, the games our governments can play. Our people are dying and negotiations are producing nothing," Aaron said. "We need help. We need to know what the Russians are up to and what type of arms they are supplying the Arabs. You know if the governments stayed out and just let people like you and I do our jobs, we would have peace. But, what do I know, I'm just…"

"Yeah, yeah, yeah. You're just an old man with seven grandchildren. I've heard that one before,

Aaron," Tom replied shaking his head. He knew Aaron was right about the games the governments played with each other.

"Listen, I can't promise anything, but I will see what I can do. But, if you ever send another agent to within one hundred feet of my secretary again, so help me Aaron I will cut off the information flow to Israel permanently," Tom added forcefully.

"Our agent hasn't returned to Israel yet. So, how did you know this secretary was approached?" Aaron smiled.

"She was on to him right from the start, for God's sake," Tom sneered. "What kind of bumbling agents are you hiring now days, Aaron? No wonder you guys are in such a mess."

"Our agent is young," Aaron explained. "He will undergo more training when he returns. As you know, it takes time to reach our level of experience. Tom, I want to thank you for anything you can give us," Aaron said turning serious. "For everything we had in place, the Egyptians came out of the blue and took us by surprise on this one. That can't happen to us again. So, thank you, my old friend. I miss our days in the field," he said sincerely.

"Yeah, well. Like I said, I'll see what I can do," added Tom.

"My best to your wife and family, Tom."

"Yeah, and my best to your seven grandchildren, you old weasel," Tom snorted as he hung up the phone.

Aaron Zucker was smiling as he gently replaced the receiver. He opened the top drawer of the desk and took out his pipe and tobacco pouch. He began to chuckle as he filled the bowl and tamped the tobacco down. When he had it lit, he leaned back in his chair and whispered to himself, "I wonder how long it will take Tom to figure out it was him we wanted to make contact with all along. We used his secretary to get to him. Too bad, David will never know the whole truth about his first mission. But, he's young. He has a lot to learn about this business of ours." He watched the smoke rise in the air.

As Tom was driving back to Langley, he realized he hadn't had lunch yet. He was busy trying to figure out how he was going to get the information to the Mossad.

"I'll see if I can spot a McDonalds," he muttered as he drove.

I want to try that new thing, a Big Mac. See if it's any good. An interesting concept those arches, he thought as he spotted the restaurant a block away. He read somewhere that McDonalds was the best marketing company in the U.S. today.

By the time he arrived in the parking lot and got out of his car, his mind was back to the problem of getting information to the Israelis. He entered the restaurant and got in line to place his order. While watching the hustle and bustle behind the counter, questions ran through his mind.

Why the hell did the Mossad send that raw recruit on such an important mission? I understand he had to be young in order to relate to Connie, but why the doofus? They had to know she would be on to him, which she was. And, like all spy organizations, she had to report the meeting.

Once he got his Big Mac, he left the restaurant and walked to his car. He smiled in satisfaction. At least, I made it clear to Aaron that Connie was off limits to them when I called him.

Then he stopped in his tracks. "Son of a bitch," Tom said out loud. Connie wasn't the primary target, he thought. It was me all along that Aaron needed to make contact with.

And, I played right into your hands with my phone call to you. You sly, old fox. He started laughing uproariously.

CHAPTER 9

Nicholas was sitting in a Moscow café reading the latest edition of *Pravda* while having a cup of tea. He folded the newspaper so the last page was facing up when he finished the tea. After leaving the paper on the table, he walked out into the morning sun. It was the beginning of July. Nicholas' favorite time of year called *White Nights,* because the sun shone for approximately eighteen hours a day. But, not for long, he thought. Soon it would be September and the rains would come. From then on, the sky would remain cloudy almost everyday until the snow started falling in late November. By December there would be no sunshine, because the sun sitting so low on the horizon for only a little over six hours a day would cause the day to merely dim. And, the people would live in darkness for the other eighteen hours.

Shortly after Nicholas left the café, another patron walked over to the table vacated by him and retrieved the newspaper he had left behind. The patron sat down and proceeded to read it cover to cover. But, when he finished reading, he tucked the paper under his arm and left the café.

On his way back to work, Nicholas walked through Gorky Park located in heart of Moscow on the banks of the Moskva River. Three hundred and forty acres set aside for this beautiful park and very few benches to sit on to enjoy it, Nicholas thought. The government took the majority of the benches out so the Soviet citizens could not congregate lest there be subversive discussions.

Ah, my beloved country. How did we get here? The more he worked with the Americans, the more he was convinced all people in espionage were nuts. And, the KGB had to top them all in paranoia. At one point at the Academy, he was given the choice of continuing his military studies or switching to the KGB. Thank goodness, he made the right choice. How can you live your daily life always thinking everyone was an enemy? Everyone was a traitor? How can you possibly see the good in people?

To carry on this game to topple Igor, Nicholas had to change the methods of passing information to the Americans every two weeks! This was the last time he would be using the newspaper to underline words in invisible ink. The next time, the Americans wanted him to leave the message inside a used soup can at the designated drop point. And, that was another thing. The drop point was different each and every time. By the time this was over, they would have him running all over Moscow. What have I gotten myself into?

Nicholas started to shake his head and smile, but stopped it as quick as he could. One did not smile when walking alone on the streets in the Soviet Union. If you did, people thought you were crazy and reported you. Other than the KGB, no citizen ever made direct eye contact with another person either. You kept to yourself with your head down. Ach, enough of these thoughts.

It is time I had some fun again. Tonight, I am going to the tavern with Andre, Nicholas thought in anticipation. He and his friend had not seen each other for over two years. Tonight couldn't come soon enough. Andre said the girls would be beautiful. I have been sad long enough. I am going to dance and drink and laugh. The hell with tomorrow or next week, he thought as he stopped to buy a bouquet of flowers for his secretary's Name Day.

"Remember, General Polakova wants you to attend a strategy meeting at eleven this morning," Nicholas' secretary told him when he entered his office and gave her the flowers.

"Happy Name Day, Olga," Nicholas said. "By the way, have you finished preparing the copies of my report for the meeting?"

"Of course. They are on your desk, Comrade," she said as she reached behind her desk for a vase. And, just as efficiently with a slight smile and a nod of her head she added, "Thank you for the flowers."

At eleven o'clock, Igor began the meeting with a review of the Soviet military postings in the Soviet Union. He stressed the importance of maintaining the heaviest postings along the Western fronts due to any increased build up of the NATO forces in Europe.

Because he came from the old school of thought, Igor could not see the future beyond the Cold War with the West, thought Nicholas. What a short-sighted fool he was. We also need to control the Islamists in the South, because sooner or later, they are going to present a problem. Just Chechnya alone is already causing headaches. The Chechen people were afraid of nothing.

After the other members of the panel had given their reports that simply mirrored Igor's sentiments, he called on Nicholas for his report.

Nicholas handed each member a copy of his research and began his presentation. It included a review of the military strength in all of the Soviet Union. He pointed out the fact that the military needed more presences in the southern and east-ern parts of the USSR, since it was here the army was at its weakest.

"Until we are able to develop ways to get at the oil in Siberia and be self-sustaining, we must be ready to move on short notice in the Middle East," he said as he ended his report. All members responded favorably to his research.Igor smiled as he thanked Nicholas for the hard work.

But, Igor was furious as he went back to his office after the meeting. "I am sick of this punk always trying to undermine me," Igor fumed under his breath. Now that Ilena is dead, I don't have to worry about her spoiled son. I need to get rid of him. The sooner, the better. I have assigned an agent to watch him. I need to call the agent to see if contact has been made.

CHAPTER 10

Connie looked at the six outfits arranged on her bed. For the past hour she had been trying to decide which one to wear for her big date with Richard Morgan tonight. According to the color chart in the woman's magazine she bought – Red is adventurous. Black is sexy. Green or blue is fun loving. And, tan or gray is demure.

"Oh, I don't know which one to choose, " she fumed. "Okay, first, I am going to get rid of the tan and gray outfits. My grandmother wore those colors for heaven's sake. Then, I am going to flip a coin to eliminate the others," she announced as she took a quarter out of her purse. "Heads, the red one is out; tails, the blue one is out."

Tails. "Hang up the blue outfit," she said as she put the tan, beige, and blue ones back in her closet.

She turned to the three remaining ones still on the bed – red, green and black. This is silly. When in doubt wear black. Besides, she liked the black skirt and cropped jacket top. Sexy, schmexy. He probably won't even notice what I am wearing.

At seven o'clock on the dot, the buzzer rang. It was Richard. Connie buzzed to let him into the building; checked herself one more time in the mirror next to the door; took a deep breath and let it out as she answered his knock on her door.

"Hi, Richard. You said seven and seven it is," she smiled as she stepped aside as he entered.

"I am punctual to a fault. You look very nice tonight, Connie," Richard said as he looked at her.

Wow, he did notice.

"Shall we go?" Richard said as he helped her with her coat. He took her arm as they walked to the elevator. "Oh, by the way, we won't be going into Georgetown tonight. Since you live out here, I made a reservation for a restaurant near here. Why waste time driving all the way down to Georgetown?"

Oh, Connie thought, too bad, because I am dressed for Georgetown. I wonder why he changed his mind.

When they arrived at the restaurant, they were seated at a table next to the window. After the waiter set their drinks down and took their dinner order, Richard raised his glass.

"Here's looking at you, kid."

"Oh, I love *Casablanca*. I watch it every time it's shown on TV. I know all the words by heart," Connie smiled as she raised her glass and added, "We'll always have Paris."

"How did you end up working for the CIA, Richard?" Connie asked as she set her drink down.

"Well, let's see. I graduated from Princeton and the on-campus recruiter made it seem like the place to be. It was either that or my college deferment was up; and, I would have been eligible for the draft. I couldn't see myself walking through rice paddies for two years," he said.

Connie winced when Richard said that. She thought about Sandy's boyfriend, Rick who was in Vietnam. He may not like the rice paddies, but he was there.

"What about you? What it's like working for Tom Bursak?" Richard asked.

"An unbiased opinion? I think I lucked out and got the best boss in the Russian Sector. I enjoy going to work every morning." Connie replied.

"Quite a job you have, Connie. Being so close to the big boss, you must know everything that happens in the entire department. Do you have trouble keeping all those secrets?" he asked quietly as he looked out the window.

Connie frowned. None of her friends at the CIA had ever asked her a question like that before. "Oh, I don't think of myself in that way. As far as secret . . . I don't know, Richard. It's just the way life is in this job."

"Speaking of secrets, did Tom say anything about the pictures of the new guy, Gregorovich?" Richard watched her as he asked that question.

Connie thought back to the other day when she first got a look at those pictures. Tom wanted them to be added to the eyes-only file. She opened the envelope to check the number of photos to be filed. As she began to look through them, she stopped and caught her breath when she came to the close up of Nicholas Gregorovich's face as he was looking at an old man. His smile contained such kindness. There was such love in his eyes as he gazed at the older man. Good grief. This wasn't a spy! This was someone she felt she could trust and depend on.

She held that picture up to show her boss. "Tom, this man cannot possibly be a spy. Look at his face. The gentleness. He is much too kind."

"I knew it. The minute I saw the picture, I knew you would say something like that, Connie." Tom shook his head. "Give me those pictures."

He shuffled through them until he got to the one of Nicholas's face showing pure hatred as he was looking at his stepfather. Tom slid that one across his desk.

"Take a look at this. Now tell me about his gentleness? This is the reason he wants to be a spy. Apparently, he found out his stepfather had his father killed during the War. He wants revenge against him. And, he's willing to do anything to get it."

Connie dismissed the photo of Nicholas looking at Igor Polakova. "I don't care what you think. This man has the capacity for kindness and love. Trust me on this, Tom." Connie smiled as she remembered how Tom put his head down and groaned when she said that.

"Tom said that Gregorovich hasn't any love," she said with a slight smile.

Richard just stared at Connie as if he didn't understand what she said.

After the awkward moment passed, the rest of the evening flew by. The conversation flowed easily between them. Connie told him about life at Boston

College where she got her degree, her love of jazz and spy novels. Richard told her about growing up in Connecticut and going to Princeton.

Once back at Connie's apartment, Richard insisted on walking her to her apartment door. Oh, here we go. Do I or don't I ask him in, Connie thought as they stepped into the elevator. She needed to break the silence.

"Richard, are you free next Saturday night? I have two tickets to the Ella Fitzgerald concert at the National Cultural Center."

"Oh, I'm sorry, Connie. I have plans to go home to my parents' house next weekend. It's my mother's birthday. We have a tradition of always getting together for birthdays. However, are you free next Friday? If you like jazz, there's a club in the downtown area that features local artists. I can pick you up at seven again," he said as the doors slid open.

Connie took the keys out of her purse as they walked to her door. "That sounds terrific. I'd like that."

It was Richard who solved the "do I or don't I" dilemma. At her door, he bent his head and kissed her softly on the lips. He kept his arms around her waist and smiled.

"I had a very nice time tonight. I don't think there was one time you gave only one word responses," he teased. "I'm looking forward to next week."

Connie stepped out of his arms and unlocked her door. When she entered, she turned to face him. "I had a good time too. Thank you. I'll see you next Friday at seven. Sounds like a movie title, doesn't it? "Friday Night at Seven"," she smiled.

He leaned against the doorframe and put his hand on her face. "You know, Connie, it might be a good idea at work not to mention the fact we're seeing each other. I don't care for gossip. I don't like people talking about me."

For a split second, Connie said nothing. Of course, she had no intention of saying anything about their dating. She couldn't stand office gossip either. But, for some reason, it hurt when he put it into words. It was as if he was ashamed of her.

"No, don't worry, Richard. I like my privacy too."

"Good," he said as he kissed her again. "Friday Night at Seven then." He raised his eyebrow as he backed away and then turned toward the elevator.

Connie leaned back against the closed door of her apartment. What an unusual date that was, she thought. He is so good-looking and classy. I had such a good time with him. And, yet several times tonight things got weird – like asking me about the secrets I knew and what was the question about pictures of Gregorovich all about? Ah, well, maybe it is just the nature of our professions. We read too much into every little thing.

As Richard was waiting for the elevator, he thought about what Connie said when he asked her about the Gregorovich pictures. He doesn't have any love? What kind of dumb answer was that? Well, at least Bursak didn't make a big deal about the fact I by-passed my boss when I brought the photos to him first.

I have more questions for Connie. And, next time, I have no intention of saying good night at her door either, Richard thought as he stepped into the elevator.

CHAPTER 11

Nicholas sat back in his chair, his legs stretched out in front of him as he listened to the small combo playing traditional Russian music. This was the life – a glass of vodka and the strumming of a balalaika. Whether a person was in a massive concert hall or in a small café like this one, Russian music touched one's very soul.

When Nicholas and his friend walked into the café tonight, they were immediately surrounded by their comrades from the military. He hadn't seen some of them since his days at the Academy. The shouting and bear hugs were just like old times.

How long have I been gone, he thought as someone handed him another vodka. I am glad Andre talked me into coming with him tonight.

Andre turned to his friend. "So, Nicholas, what have you been up to the past two years? I hear you are still working for your stepfather. I don't know how you do it. I'm surprised you haven't shot him yet."

Well, Andre certainly broke the mood with his comments. I can't even enjoy a simple evening out without being on my guard. Once I made the decision to work with the Americans, my life changed, Nicholas thought. I now lead two, very distinct lives. And, hard as I try, I can't escape the fact that I have become a spy. I hope this ends soon. I want to be done and over with this business and get back to normal. Maybe it will never happen, he reflected.

Nicholas shook his head to get rid of those thoughts and smiled at his friend. "It's not so bad, Andre. I just do my job and try to stay out of Igor's way. How are you doing working with supporting the troops in the Eastern Bloc countries?"

Andre sneered, "The same old story – too many shortages. We need more guns, more ammunition, more uniforms, more everything. My boss is screaming at me to find more supplies. The factories are screaming at me that they are working as hard as they can. Some days I hate to go to work. Ah, well, this is Russia, nothing changes."

The combo began to play the Russian Folk tune, *Kalinka*. Andre and two of his comrades at the table grabbed Nicholas and dragged him toward the dance floor.

"Come on, Comrade. Here is where we impress the women with our dancing skills." Andre smiled as he put his arm around Nicholas' shoulder to begin the dance.

Nicholas had just enough to drink to make dancing seem like a good idea. They stood in a line and began bowing down on one leg as they slapped the other leg out to the side on the beat. Back up, they changed directions, and went the other way . . . *Ka-lin-ka, Ka-lin-ka, Ka-lin-ka.* The patrons joined in singing and emphasizing the beat. As the tempo picked up, the men stood, grabbed each other's shoulders and danced furiously laughing all the while. At the end of the song, everyone cheered as the men left the dance floor.

"Ah, Andre, I am so glad we met up again and you talked me into coming with you tonight," Nicholas said as he sat down. He refilled their glasses and raised his.

"*Nahz Drovya,* old friend."

Andre raised his glass. "To old times. We have to do this more often. Let us try to get together at least once a week. We cannot let the years go by again."

"By the way, now that we have dazzled the ladies, we have to act like peacocks as they admire us," Andre laughed as he leaned back in his chair checking out the women as he looked around the café.

"You haven't changed a bit, Andre. You are still the same randy goat you always were."

"Why, Nicholas, I do believe there is one young lady who would like to rip your clothes off. See the dark haired one across the room who can't seem to take her eyes off of you." Andre pointed across the room. "I know her. Her name is Katrina. She works in the same building with me. She has quite a reputation. This is your night, you lucky son-of-a-gun."

Nicholas looked in the direction Andre was pointing. The woman was looking directly at him and Andre was right. There was no doubt in the woman's eyes as to what she was offering. Even with the liquor, that was too blatant for him. There was something to be said for the chase.

Without taking her eyes off of Nicholas, the woman leaned slightly and said something to her friend sitting next to her. The other young woman turned and looked at Nicholas. She had blond hair and dark eyes. She raised her eyes and gazed at him without guile. She gave him a slight smile and turned away. He sucked in his breath. She was so beautiful, like an angel. He couldn't take his eyes off of her. Nicholas was intrigued with her. Nothing like this ever happened to him before. He stood up.

He grabbed Andre by the arm. "I want to meet her."

"So, it has been that long since you got laid? Don't worry, Katrina will give it to you any time, anywhere." Andre looked surprised as his friend dragged him out of his chair.

"No. Not her, you fool – the other one sitting next to her. Besides, Katrina is more your type not mine," he hissed.

"Good evening, ladies. May my friend and I join you?" Nicholas said as he pulled out the chair next to the "angel" never taking his eyes off her. "My name is Nicholas and this is my friend Andre."

"I am Katrina and this is my friend Anya." If Katrina was disappointed Nicholas chose Anya, she didn't show it. She turned her attention to Andre. "So we meet at last. I have seen you at work, Comrade."

Andre preened. "How could you not notice me?"

Once Nicholas heard her name, Anya, he tuned out everything else. As far as he was concerned, there was just the two of them. He wanted to know everything he could about her.

As they talked, he learned her mother had been Finish and her father Russian. The blond hair came from her mother, the dark eyes from her father. Because both her parents were no longer living, she now lived with her Russian grandmother. She had an engineering degree and was a manager at the electric company.

The combo switched from Russian Folk songs to modern music. "Would you like to dance, Anya?" Nicholas asked as he smiled at her. He held her hand and led her onto the dance floor. When he took her in his arms, it seemed their bodies fit perfectly.

After the song ended, they went back to their table. Andre and Katrina had disappeared.

"It looks like our friends have left us," Nicholas said. "Do you want to wait for your friend to return?"

"No. I might as well go home. Katrina does have a tendency to forget about me sometimes. Thank you Nicholas. I'm glad I met you," Anya said as she gathered her coat and purse.

Nicholas also rose. "I will see you home, Anya." He definitely did not want this night to end.

When he left her at her door, they made plans to spend the next day together.

CHAPTER 12

The plane was still over the Mediterranean as it began its decent into Israel. David looked out the window at the multiple shades of blue of the Sea. It was morning and the sun was just above the horizon. The view was breathtaking, but not for him.

"My first assignment, and I blew it. Too bad I couldn't jump out of the plane right now and be done with it," David whispered. He dreaded having to face the Mossad about his failure in Washington. He could see it now. He would forever be branded as the agent with the shortest tenure in the Mossad. But, what hurt him most was the fact he had let Aaron down.

Well, it was time to act like a man and face the music, he thought as the plane came to a stop next to the terminal. He got his small, duffel bag from the overhead compartment and proceeded down the aisle into the building. When he reached the gate area, he stopped in his tracks. There was Aaron Zucker! He was standing there alone with his hands in his pockets waiting. He looked like the most unassuming old man in his rumpled, dark suit. What an act that was. David smiled to himself. Aaron had the sharpest mind in the entire Mossad. He forgot nothing – even the smallest detail did not escape him.

"Shalom, David."

"Aaron! What are you doing here?"

"I came to welcome you home, My Boy. Come, I have my car."

David groaned. Smart he might be, but Aaron's driving was notorious. He drove like a maniac. It was rumored he crashed at least nine vehicles during his days in the field.

"Just as well I didn't bother jumping out over the Mediterranean. I'm going to be killed on the way home anyway. At least I won't have to explain my failure to Aaron," David muttered as he shouldered his duffel bag and followed his mentor.

As the car screeched to a halt outside the Mossad building, David instinctively put his hand out to stop his forward movement. He flew forward toward the dash and then boomeranged back into his seat again. When he opened the door his knees were so weak, he nearly fell out of the car.

"For god's sake, Aaron. Don't you know how to stop a car? What are you trying to do? And, you nearly hit three cars with all that swerving." His voice was an octave higher than normal.

"Ah, but the secret is, I didn't hit any of them." Aaron strolled away completely oblivious to the whiteness of David's face.

Once in his office, Aaron indicated David should take a seat in front of his desk. He folded his hands in front of him and looked David in the eye.

"I am going to do the debriefing of your assignment in Washington. I will need all the facts from the moment you landed in D.C. until you took off again. You may begin," he said as he took a note pad and pencil out of his desk.

"I blew it, Aaron. I let you down," David said with anguish.

"I'll be the judge of that. Continue."

Slowly, David began. This was so difficult for him. He kept his eyes down and his hands clasped on his thighs. He left nothing out – even the kiss.

When he finished, he finally looked up. Aaron was holding his head in his hands. The pencil lay on the note pad. He had ceased writing minutes ago.

"My God, David. For all the training you received, I don't think there was one thing you managed to do right," Aaron said quietly. "And, here you were the one who was worried about the Mossad prostituting you. The only good thing is that you kept it in your pants."

David winced. However, he wasn't about to tell Aaron, he wouldn't have kept it in his pants if Connie hadn't stopped him.

Aaron finally raised his head and looked up at David. "For what it is worth, we are getting the information we need from the Americans."

David was bewildered. "I don't understand. You did get the information from the Americans? Who gave it to you? Certainly, not Connie."

"Her boss, Tom Bursak, is giving us what we need. And, why don't you know this? I thought you said, Connie told you she was going to speak to her boss."

"Ah, yeah. About that," David cleared his throat. "I didn't wait. I was so embarrassed about failing, I made arrangements and left Washington early the next morning."

"Oy vey," Aaron said as he lowered his head back in hands again. He finally looked up shaking his head. "As strange as it may seem, and I may regret this, I happen to think you have the ability and the tools to become a good agent for Israel. But, before you do anything else, you are going to be subjected to another round of very, intense training. No way will you be given another assignment without that."

"One more thing, David. Why did you tell this secretary who you were? Why did you tell her everything, you idiot?"

"She was just so nice and easy to talk to," David said softly.

"She was the enemy!" Aaron screamed. "Every single contact is always the enemy. You are going to grow up. Never again, are you going to act like this in the field," Aaron yelled. "Never again, are you going to act this stupid!" He pointed a finger at David and then slammed his fist on the desk.

CHAPTER 13

Igor Polakova made two phone calls before he left his office for the night. The first call was to his mistress, Helena, telling her he would be arriving in one hour. She was young and beautiful. She met all his sexual needs flawlessly. But, from the first night he was with her, Helena made it very clear that he must always call before coming to her apartment. For all Igor's power, she was the one person he could not intimidate. He tried to threaten her once. She just laughed at him then refused to see him for two weeks. He had to beg her to take him back. He hated this weakness in himself. But, he was consumed with her, so he made the phone call.

The second phone call was very important. It was to the agent he had assigned to watch Nicholas. The person answered on the second ring. Without introducing himself, Igor merely said, "Have you made contact with Gregorovich yet?"

There was a slight pause. "Yes, I have made contact."

"And? What have you learned? What did he say about me?"

The other person answered, "Gregorovich said the normal things that everyone else says about you, Comrade."

Igor was already fuming over his required phone call to his mistress. This insubordination he would not tolerate.

"Watch your mouth, Comrade. I told you if you failed in this assignment, you and your family would end up in Siberia. One more flippant comment like that, and I won't bother with Siberia. I'll just make you and your family disappear for good. Are we clear, Comrade," Igor said menacingly.

"Yes," the person answered quietly.

Igor nodded his head as he realized his threat had been understood. "I want you to stick with Gregorovich. Try to get him to talk about himself – where he goes, what he does. Learn everything you can about him.

"I will be calling you every week at this time for an update. Make sure you are available." Igor hung up the phone without waiting for an answer.

CHAPTER 14

"Richard, how did you ever find this place? It's fantastic," Connie asked while clapping enthusiastically as the last jazz trio of the evening ended their set with "Take the A-Train".

"I saw a review for this club in the *Washington Post* last month. It's been opened for five months now and features only local talent. I have to agree with you. It is fantastic. I didn't know D.C. had such incredible talent," Richard answered.

Connie was still smiling as she stood up to leave. "Well, I must say tonight was the best Friday Night at Seven date ever. Thank you so much," she said as she was putting on her coat.

Standing behind her, he put his hands on her shoulders. "Thank you, Connie. I would never have thought of coming here, if you hadn't mentioned you liked jazz."

As they drove back to Connie's apartment, Richard kept his eyes on the road while he spoke. "Connie, I am trying to keep track of where my boss is during the day in case something important comes up and I have to get a hold of him in a hurry. He doesn't always let me know where he is. Would you call me and let me know whenever Jeff is in a meeting with Tom?"

Connie didn't know what to say to that. She could understand why Richard felt it was necessary to know Jeff's whereabouts, but telling him about any meetings with Tom would be a violation of trust with Tom. And, there was no way she would ever do something like that.

"Well, Richard, I think you could get that information from Jeff's secretary, Francine." Trying to be diplomatic without hurting Richard's feelings, she added, "She's the one who would know Jeff's schedule during the day."

He did not look pleased with her answer. Here we go again, she thought. Another great evening and then Richard comes out with some weird question. Maybe I shouldn't be dating someone from the office.

When they reached her apartment door, Connie took the keys from her purse and unlocked the door. She turned to say goodnight. Richard looked at her and said, "Why don't you invite me in?"

"Oh. Ah . . .okay."

She walked through the door and turned on the wall light. I'm sure he just wants a cup of coffee, right? On the other hand, maybe not. The question is what do I want. Him, definitely, him. On the other hand, maybe not. Oh, I hate these awkward moments with a passion.

"Would you like something to drink? I have coffee, soda or brandy," she asked as she hung up their coats.

"A brandy sounds good. Would you mind if I looked at your record collection while you get our drinks?" Richard asked as he walked to the record cabinet.

"Not at all. I have jazz, of course, then an eclectic mix of records from college. I know I need to buy a bigger music cabinet to store everything. Music is another of my weaknesses." Connie went to the kitchen to pour the drinks.

As she picked up the brandy snifters and was returning to the living room, she heard Frank

Sinatra begin to sing. Oh, no, she thought. Someone at work once mentioned listening to Frank Sinatra records was responsible for half the babies born in the U.S. in the last twenty years. She hoped her hands weren't shaking as she placed the glasses on her coffee table. She had to sit down quickly before her legs gave out.

After a few minutes, Richard set his glass down and removed the snifter from Connie's hand. "Let's dance," he said as he stood and held out his hand to her.

Frank started singing "I've Got You Under My Skin".

This feels so good Connie thought as Richard held her close and began swaying.

I've got you under my skin. I've got you deep in the heart of me.

Oh, my goodness, Connie thought as Richard began kissing her cheek, her eyes and her neck.

So deep in my heart, you're really a part of me.

And, his tongue. What is he doing with his tongue?

I've got you under my skin.

Oh, my gosh. Now we're dancing toward my bedroom door. I can't think when he's doing to those things with his hands.

Don't you know little fool? You never can win. Wake up to reality. Use your mentality.

Good grief. Is that my blouse on the floor? How did that get there? And, my bra! Where's my bra? I'm sure I had one on tonight, didn't I?

But, each time I do, just the thought of you makes me stop before I begin, because, I've got you under my skin.

By the time, they got through the door, both had their clothes off and neither of them heard the song end as they whipped the bed spread and blankets out of the way and fell onto Connie's bed. What started out as quiet, seductive foreplay now turned into frantic urgency as they brought each other to a frenzied climax.

When they were done, neither had the strength to move. They continued to hold each other. Just breathing took an effort. Finally, they began to stir. Richard reached over for the sheet and blanket to cover Connie, but rather than covering himself too, he got up and started to pick up his clothes.

"Richard, you don't have to leave," Connie smiled. "You're welcome to stay until morning. After what just happened, I feel I at least owe you a breakfast," she chuckled.

He looked at Connie over his shoulder as he was sitting on her bed putting on his socks. "No. I had better leave now. I don't think it would be a good idea for me to be seen leaving your apartment in the morning." He saw the hurt look on her face as he said this.

"What would your neighbors think?" he said trying to mollify her. "And, besides, I will be leaving early in the morning for the weekend."

Connie got up and went to her closet for her robe. "Well, have fun at your party," she said as she put it on.

"My what?" he asked.

She turned and looked at him questioningly. "Your mother's birthday party. Last Friday you said you were going to your mother's birthday party this weekend."

"Oh, yeah. You're right. I'm sorry. I just never think of her birthday as having fun. More of an obligation, really." He stuffed his tie into his jacket pocket.

As they walked out of the bedroom together, Connie realized the record player was still on and the needle was going back and forth at the end of the record. She went to shut it off. At Connie's door, he kissed her and said, "I'll call you Monday night if that's all right? I had a good time tonight, Connie, and I want to see you again."

What is it with Richard, Connie thought as she closed the door. Almost everything was perfect tonight. But, then something screwy happened again. He actually thought I would let him know when Jeff was in a meeting with Tom. And worse yet – why did he act so odd when I mentioned his mother's birthday? How can anyone think his mother's birthday was an *obligation*? I would give anything to be able to celebrate a birthday with my mother again.

On the way to the elevator, Richard thought about Connie mentioning his mother's birthday party. Well one thing I learned tonight, Connie never forgets a detail. I'm going to have to be very careful what I tell her from now on. And, then remember what I told her.

Walking out to his car, Richard thought about his date tonight. I really did have a good time tonight. And, I really do want to see her again. Watch it, Morgan. Get those thoughts out of your head. You have a plan, and she's not in it.

CHAPTER 15

Anya, Anya, Anya. I could say her name a hundred times a day and never get tired, Nicholas thought as he daydreamed at his desk. Since he met her last Friday, he and Anya managed to spend time together every single day this past week. Last night, they joined Andre and his date at the café where they had met. Of course, Andre being Andre was with another new girl yet again. I don't know how he does it with a different girl very time. I couldn't do it.

Tonight he would be meeting Anya's grandmother for the first time. The three of them were going to have dinner together at Anya's apartment. He needed to bring the grandmother something special to make a good first impression and get on her good side. Nothing is worse than having a grumpy, Russian grandmother. I think I will buy her some chocolates. That should do it.

During his lunch hour, Nicholas walked over to the officer's only military store for chocolates and flowers. One of the perks of putting up with working for Igor – he got to shop at that store. It had few if any shortages. And, one didn't have to stand in those horrible long lines waiting for one lousy loaf of bread. Someone told him, in a whisper, of course, that in America every city, big or small, had huge grocery stores where people actually pushed large carts around to hold all their goods. He didn't believe it though. That couldn't be possible. Maybe some day, he would be able to travel outside of the Soviet Union to see if that was true. When though? Today, the government allowed very, very few Soviet citizens to travel beyond its borders. Those who did travel were usually diplomats or high-ranking military people only.

This was a good day at the military store. Nicholas had three kinds of chocolate to choose from. He bought the grandmother the biggest box. That should make her happy, he smiled. And, he bought Anya a bouquet of flowers.

In the early evening, Nicholas parked his car near Anya's apartment. He took one last look at himself in the rearview mirror to make sure he looked presentable – hair combed and nothing stuck in his teeth or mustache. He retrieved the candy and flowers from the passenger seat and got out of his car. As he walked down the street, his American handler, dressed in his workingman's clothes, approached him.

"Good evening, Comrade. How is your plumbing problem? Beautiful flowers and chocolates too, must be an important date."

"Shit." Every time my life starts to bring happiness, I am slammed back into this ugly world. Why didn't I meet Anya before I contacted the Americans? Because of Anya, my hatred of Igor doesn't seem quite so bad now. If I had only met her first, I wouldn't have reacted so decisively and contacted the Americans.

I don't want to tell my handler about Anya. I cannot and will not put her life in jeopardy. I need to get out of this spy business now, so she and I have a chance to develop our relationship honestly without secrets.

"Comrade, good to see you. My plumbing problems seem to be solved. So, I won't need your services anymore." I hope he gets the subtle hint I just gave him.

"Sorry, pal. But, it doesn't work that way. We need some information, and you are going to get it for us. Remember, Nicholas, you are the one who contacted us. Once you took that step, you changed your life forever. Therefore, there is no walking away. Not now, not ever." The Handler watched the look of astonishment cross Nicholas' face as he spoke those harsh words. He continued to stare at him to make sure what he had just said was understood.

"Now, keep walking as I explain what you are to do next. We want to know what types of arms the Soviet military is selling to the Middle Eastern countries. And, we also want to know what type of military advisors the Soviet Union has in those countries. We need the information as soon as possible. In fact, we want it by next Wednesday. You are to put the information inside an empty Pepsi can and leave it on the ground next to the trash container near the eastern most bridge in Gorky Park. We suggest you make the drop after work not during your lunch hour."

"One more thing, Comrade. We watched you make the last drop. You couldn't have been more obvious. You entered the Park, walked directly to the trash container, dropped the soup can on the ground and then walked out of the Park. You couldn't have been more stupid about what you were doing," the Handler hissed. "You were lucky on that one, because as far as we could tell, you were not being followed."

Nicholas was sick to his stomach when he heard that. Who could be following him? How could anyone know? He told no one what he was doing. So far, he had not stolen any files from work. He made no photocopies of any documents. Because he was a research analyst, everything he handed over to the Americans had been the information he personally knew about or wrote papers on. Like the information about the three silos they had asked for as his first assignment. What a joke that was on the Americans. They thought we were building missile silos, but the only thing we are doing is using those silos for storing nuclear waste products. No way are we going to keep that garbage on Russian soil. Let the Estonians and Bulgarians deal with that mess.

The Handler added, "This time, act natural. Enter the Park, and stop a few times. Pretend you are drinking that Pepsi, for god sake. When you reach the trash container, stop again as if you are finishing the soda before you toss the can toward the container. Make sure it drops on the ground near it. Don't put it directly into the container. If you drop it into the container, there may be other Pepsi cans in it, and we would have to spend too much time and call too much attention to ourselves retrieving all of them."

"Nicholas, I like you. Under other circumstances, you and I would probably be friends. I'm sure of it. But, you have got to start thinking and acting like a spy. This is for your own good."

Nicholas looked at the Handler with sad eyes. "I'll get the information you want." The Handler nodded once and walked away.

He's right. I am in this, and I can't get out until Igor is destroyed. So, I must hurry the process as much as I can. I want to have my life back. I want to be able to be with Anya. I need to start thinking like a spy. How horrible, because I am not a spy. I am just trying to get vengeance for my father's murder.

CHAPTER 16

David seemed to be redeeming himself the second time around in his classes. In fact, he was glad he had the opportunity to go through the training again. Some of the classes were a repeat, like the Psychology of the Agent in the Field, but many of them were advanced and new. He was grateful to Aaron and could see his own growth as an agent. There were those who grew with their experiences in the field, and then there is me who does it in a classroom. Schmuck.

He was thinking these thoughts as he lay in his bed after a grueling day on the combat field. His nightmares were getting fewer and fewer for which he was grateful. He knew they would never go away completely, but the shock and horror of that day was receding. Strangely enough, he had new dreams that were not going away. The dreams of Connie O'Rourke kept coming back. What was it about her that made it impossible to stop thinking about her? Why was it she kept popping into his head? He thought about this as he rolled over and turned out the light.

He knew the chances of ever meeting her again were a complete zero. He wished that were not true. He never met any woman who was as comfortable to be with as Connie. He would like to know how she is and whether she felt the same way.

But, as a Mossad agent, one didn't call a contact for old time sake.

"Remember me? I was the one who tried to compromise you. I'm just calling to see how you are." Jeez.

CHAPTER 17

On Wednesday evening, Nicholas walked into Gorky Park with the can of Pepsi. Shortly after he entered, he stopped and pretended to take a drink like his handler had told him to do. His hands were shaking as he brought the can to his lips. He surreptitiously looked around to see if anyone was watching him. Nothing looked out of the ordinary.

When he started this, it all seemed so simple – get the information, hand it over to the Americans, bring Igor down – done, over, don't have to think about it anymore. Now the reality that he could be caught and tried for treason was terrifying.

He proceeded toward the bridge. When he reached the river, he stopped and leaned on the railing. Looking out at the water, he pretended to take another drink. He set the can down on a piling and held it casually with two hands as he gazed at the water. The information about the Soviet dealings in the Middle East was written on a small piece of paper wadded up inside the can. Thank goodness this was another thing he could supply without having to remove copies or documents.

"Hello, Nicholas."

"Anya!" Nicholas said as he spun around to face her. He nearly dropped the Pepsi can into the river, but caught it just in time. "What are you doing here?"

"I saw you enter the Park just now and decided to follow you. I wanted to tell you I am able to spend the weekend with you at your mother's house. I told my grandmother I would be staying at Katrina's apartment on Friday and Saturday. She seemed to accept that. Actually, I have a feeling I could have told her the truth about our plans. I think she wouldn't have a problem with it. She likes you, Nicholas," Anya grinned. "It must have been the big box of chocolates you gave her."

Nicholas smiled back at her as his heart rate began to slow down. He could hardly wait for this weekend. He wanted to show her where he grew up. But, mostly, he wanted to be alone with her.

He had already stocked his refrigerator with food, so there would be no need for them to leave the house the entire time. He wanted no distractions as he made love to her. The thought was driving him crazy.

Anya looked out at the river. "I wish we didn't have to meet Andre at the café again this Friday. Why does he insist we meet him every Friday?"

Nicholas leaned against the piling with his hand around the Pepsi can. "Let's not stay too long at the café. I know Andre keeps insisting we meet him every Friday. I wish we could get out of it entirely. But, he would be crushed if we didn't meet his new girl friend of the week. So, we will go, have a vodka, say hello to the new girl and then leave, okay?" He put his free hand around Anya's shoulder and kissed her on the cheek.

"Okay," she said as she looked into his eyes and smiled. "I'm thirsty. May I have a sip of your Pepsi," Anya said as she reached for the can.

Nicholas whipped the can away. "No. Ah, I'm sorry. I finished it all. There is none left. Come, I'll buy you a Pepsi at the street vendor." He immediately took her elbow and began leading her out of the Park.

Now what do I do now? The can was like hot coals in his hand. I need to get rid of this as soon as I can. What a close call that was. I hope I didn't scare Anya with the abruptness. The path that leads directly out of the park is a few meters up ahead. But, the trash container I am supposed to use is way over by the bridge. It will seem odd if we walk all the way over there just to toss this can away. I hope the Americans are watching me, because I am not going to use that drop point. As they walked up the closer path, Nicholas pitched the can toward the trash container. It landed inside the container not next to it as directed. Without looking back, he walked briskly out of the Park with Anya.

A young man was sitting under a tree near the bridge reading a book. What the hell just happened? What did that Gregorovich do now? Something happened with the woman he's with. Who the hell is she? And, the jerk threw the can into the trash bin. Great, now I have to go digging through garbage. Crap, this day couldn't get any worse. I should have listened to my mother. I should have become an accountant.

"So, how was your day, dear?" the Handler smirked as the young CIA agent entered his room at the Embassy.

"Shut up," he answered as he glared at his boss and dumped four Pepsi cans on his desk. "Something went wrong. The dumb idiot tossed the can in the wrong trash container. And, notice I said 'in' the container. I had to take these other three cans out too."

"And, Gregorovich met a woman in the Park. I don't think it was planned, because he seemed surprised to see her there. But, they acted like they knew each other. He kissed her. Do you know anything about her?"

The Handler tapped a pencil on his desk. "Hmm, interesting. When I approached him last week, he was carrying a box of chocolates and flowers. I asked if he had a date. Now that I think about it, he never did answer my question. What did she look like?"

"Young, blond, quite good looking about 5' 6 and 135 pounds. Oh, and she doesn't look Russian either."

"I'll put someone on him to see if she's a girlfriend.

CHAPTER 18

Connie and her father exited the Smithsonian Castle onto The Mall and headed toward the Washington Monument. They had a half an hour to walk to the White House for their personal tour.

"Dad, I'm so glad you came to Washington. I really miss doing things with you. The last time you were here was with Mom and I was eight years old. We visited the Smithsonian that time too. Remember?"

Her dad smiled at her. "I remember. You were disappointed when you saw the American flag, because it only had thirteen stars on it. You couldn't understand why there weren't 48 stars. You asked your mom if they had run out of white material."

"Yeah, well, I didn't start to study American history until I was in fourth grade. So, how was I to know?" Connie laughed. "Another vacation I remember was to Maine when we went whale watching. Have you been back up there?"

"As a matter of fact, I have. Maggie and I went up there last summer," Lee answered as he looked at his daughter. "You know, we never discussed this. Are you okay about my seeing Maggie? I loved your mother very much, but after so long, it's nice to be able to share my life with someone again. You understand that, don't you?"

Connie didn't reply for a moment. She took her dad's arm as they walked. "I didn't at first, Dad. I had a real problem with it. But, after I thought about it, I realized you have a right to be happy again. And, when I met Maggie, I saw how perfect she was for you. She is so positive; and she makes you laugh. You deserve that, Dad. I am okay now." Connie kissed her dad's cheek and gave him a wink.

Relieved, Lee smiled and said, "Now how about you, Connie-my-girl? When am I going to meet this new boyfriend of yours? You've talked about him enough. I thought Richard would be with us today."

Connie knew her dad would bring that up and cringed inside. Once again, Richard was not available for the weekend. When she had invited him to have dinner with her and her father, this time he said he had another quote hush-hush mission to go on again. She didn't understand that. Since the CIA didn't operate on U.S. soil, where can an agent always be going in just two days? Other than one Sunday evening, they had not spent a full weekend together since they began dating over a month ago. When the weekends came, Richard was always out of town on some mission or couldn't get out of some personal trip. Ding, ding. Alarm bells, kiddo. You better start paying attention. But, Richard was so fantastic to be with. He was funny, knowledge-able, kind and thoughtful. The problem was she was falling for him in a big way.

"I thought he would be with us too. But, something came up at work and he had to take care of it. Maybe next time you'll have a chance to meet him," Connie said weakly.

"Well, as your father, you know I have to check him out," Lee said as he squeezed Connie's hand. "If I were still working, I would already have run a check on him. How's that for espionage…the agent who covertly checks people out would be checked out himself."

"Not funny, Dad. If you even tried to do something like that, the National Security Agency that monitors inquiries like that would learn about it. Then they would tell us about it. And, I would be totally embarrassed trying to explain it was only my overprotective dad performing his parental duties. Ugh, just the thought of it makes me ill. No kidding, Dad. You can't even joke about a thing like that. That's the world I work in. Scary, huh?"

"You're right. It scares the hell out of me, Connie. To think my little girl is working for a big fish at the CIA. I never planned that for you at all. Thank God, women aren't allowed to be agents. I don't think I would sleep ever again," her dad said.

"Dad, you make me so furious when you say things like that. There is no reason why women can't become CIA agents except for the ignorance of men who think like you. We are just as smart as any man. And, we can do any job just as well as any man. You have got to change the way you think. We are not *the wife, the little woman,* or *the weaker sex.* The sooner you realize that the better," Connie fumed.

Fortunately for her father, they had reached the gates to the White House. Connie had heard her Dad's litany too many times now.

She knew it was coming when he began, "What is this world coming to when women think they can do a man's job? Pretty soon, women will want to be doctors or engineers or policemen, God forbid. How is it, I don't seem to be able to talk to my own daughter anymore? Thank goodness, Maggie doesn't think that way. She still believes a woman's place is in the home."

Ugh, she was sick of it. She had to sit through that speech too many times. Well, not anymore. She knew more and more women felt as she did.

"I've never been to the White House. I wonder if we will get to see President Johnson?" Lee asked trying to change the subject. "By the way, when I called Senator Kennedy's office to arrange for our tour, I just happened to mention the fact my daughter works for the CIA. I think that's why we're getting this special personalized tour."

"I doubt it. CIA secretaries don't get special personalized tours, Dad. We're only women. Those types of tours are reserved for male, field agents."

Her Dad was smart enough to keep his mouth shut and just enjoy the tour.

CHAPTER 19

It was Sunday night and Connie was alone once again. She was sitting on her patio sipping a cup of tea while she listened to the newest Nancy Wilson record Richard had given her. Ever since their first date at the jazz café in D.C., he gave her a new jazz record on their every "Friday Night at Seven" date.

As she drank her tea, she thought about the previous week. A new twist was added. Richard couldn't make their usual "Friday Night at Seven" date. His excuse this time was he had to drive to Baltimore to help his old, college roommate move into a new apartment. So, they met last Thursday night instead. Even though it was a different day, she had another fantastic time with Richard. They had driven over to the banks of the Chesapeake Bay and enjoyed a Maryland crab cake dinner at a small restaurant they had discovered. After dinner they walked hand-in-hand along the waterfront. They returned to Connie's apartment around 10:30 p.m.; had great sex; and, then Richard left . . . for the long weekend.

She set her teacup on the side table and put her head back on the chaise lounge as she looked up at the stars. "This has got to stop," she murmured. "Richard, what is going on? I know you care about me. I can see it in your eyes. Yet, you have been leaving every single weekend. What is the secret you're hiding?"

The buzzer to the outside door sounded. She smiled and whispered, "Richard." She hurried to the door and pushed the wall speaker button.

"Hello."

"Connie? It's me, Tom Bursak. Buzz me up," came the reply.

"Tom? What are you doing here?" she said as she pushed the buzzer to let him into the building. Then she opened the front door and stood in the hall waiting for the elevator to arrive.

She didn't even know Tom knew where she lived. What could he possibly want at this time of night? Oh, please don't let it be something dumb that my dad did. If he tried to check up on Richard, I will be so embarrassed trying to explain it.

The elevator seemed to take forever to arrive. When Tom stepped off and saw Connie waiting and looking worried, he said, "The elevator was up on the fifth floor. I had to wait until it came back down, before I could get on."

"Why are you here, Tom. Something is wrong. I just know it." As hard as she tried, she couldn't keep the panic out of her voice.

When he approached her, Tom took her arm and led her back into her apartment. "Come on, kiddo. Let's go inside and talk." Once inside, he led her to the couch and sat down.

Still standing, Connie said, "I'm not going to like this, am I?"

"Yes and no," Tom answered as he patted the place next to him. "Sit," he said.

After she was seated, Tom said, "I have two things to tell you. First, the head of the CIA station at the Russian embassy in Moscow is going on long-term medical leave and probably won't be assigned there when he returns. I have decided to take his position for the short term while we find a permanent replacement for him. The assignment should last about three or four months at the most. I want you to go with me to Moscow." He stopped and waited for the explosion from Connie.

"Are you serious? Why would you do that? I don't understand. I don't know if I should leave my dad. Where would I live in Moscow? In an apartment? At the embassy? And, what do I do with this apartment? When would we have to leave? I don't know what to say."

"You've been doing a good job of speaking so far," Tom said as he smiled at her. "Okay – answers to your questions. Yes, I am serious. Why? Once a field agent, always a field agent. I'm going to be retiring in two years. I started my career in the OSS during World War II spying on the Russians. It has always been the Russians with me. And, this is my last chance to get back in the field, or as close as I can get to being back in the field even for a short time."

"Leaving your dad? Didn't you tell me he now has a girlfriend? He won't be alone. This is just a short assignment, Connie. I bet your father will be happy for you."

"As to the rest of your questions – you will be living in an apartment. Jennie and I will live in the

Embassy or close to it. You won't have to give up this apartment. The CIA will cover your rent while we're over there. And, we leave in two weeks. I am expected to be in Moscow by the 25th of this month."

"The 25th! Tom, I . . . I don't have an answer for you," Connie said slowly. "This is a complete shock."

"Think it over tonight and give me your decision tomorrow. I really do want you to come with me, Connie. We're a team."

Connie leaned back on the sofa. "All right, Tom. I'll let you know tomorrow." She sat forward preparing to rise then stopped. "Wait a minute." She turned to look at Tom. "You said you had two things to tell me. What's the other one?" she asked.

"Connie," Tom hesitated. "Richard Morgan got married this weekend," he said as he watched her intently.

Connie sucked in a breathe of air then the color drained from her face as she let it out. She stared straight ahead, but saw nothing. Her heart began pounding; and, she could hear the throbbing as the blood pulsed in her head. Tom continued to speak, but she didn't hear a word he said. It was as if the world ceased to exist and she was alone in a complete void.

Slowly, the room came into focus again. She realized Tom was shaking her and calling her name.

"Connie! Look at me." He immediately released her as she turned to face him.

She licked her lips and started to slowly breath in and out. "How did you know Richard and I were seeing each other?"

"I had a twenty-four hour surveillance put on him for the last six weeks."

Connie frowned. "Why?"

"I never felt comfortable with him. I needed to know why. I discussed it with his boss. We decided to see if he was up to something. As it turns out, the only thing he's guilty of is being an asshole." Tom snorted as he looked at the floor. "I came here tonight, because I wanted you to hear this from me. I didn't want you to come to work tomorrow and be taken by surprise. I'm really sorry about this, Connie," Tom said as he raised his head and looked at her again.

"How many people know about us, Tom?"

"Ah…just Jeff Evans, the three FBI guys and me."

She lowered her face in her hands and shook her head back and forth. "I've been a complete fool. I was in love with him, you know," Connie said.

Strange, no tears. But, she could feel rage building just under the surface. She dropped her hands to her sides and looked back at Tom.

"Tell me the rest of it, Tom." Her eyes were now narrow slits and her lips were pressed tightly together.

"Yesterday, Richard married Mary Elizabeth Williams from Providence, Rhode Island. She comes from old money. Her father is a behind-the-scenes mover and shaker in Washington. Eisenhower appointed him Ambassador to Argentina in the fifties," Tom said quietly as he raised and dropped his hand in a helpless gesture.

They remained quiet for a short time. Finally, Connie said, "I'll go with you to Moscow. But, I can't come in to work tomorrow. I just can't, Tom."

"I understand. Look, why don't you take some vacation time? You've always said you wanted to go to Paris. Go there for a week. When you come back, we'll only have another week before we leave for Moscow. And, don't worry. You won't have to see Richard again before we leave. He is going to Mexico for three weeks on his honeymoon. Ah, I shouldn't have added that part. I'm sorry," Tom said after he saw the look on her face.

Connie stood up and walked to the door. "I will take some time off. And, Paris might be just what I need. Thanks for telling me this in person, Tom." She stood with her hand on the doorknob.

"Connie, are you going to be all right? Should I call my wife, Jennie to come and stay with you?" he asked as he walked to the door.

"I'll be okay. Don't worry. This is my problem and I have to deal with it." She opened the door indicating that Tom should leave.

After he left, she wandered over to the windows and stood looking out on the night. She thought of all those excuses for the weekends when he couldn't be here. This weekend he had the gall to say he had to help his cousin move! But, the worst one is he made love to me two nights before his wedding. What a horrible, ugly, vile human being he is. And, what a pathetic, idiotic loser I am. She sank down to the floor, turned on her side and began to sob uncontrollably.

CHAPTER 20

I made the right decision to come to Paris Connie thought as she was sitting at an outdoor café. The sun was warm this time of year in France. It felt good on her skin. She raised her face to the sun and closed her eyes. For the very first time in three days, she did not think about the pain Richard had caused. She found herself, not smiling yet, but on the verge of peace.

I know the pain will come back, she thought. But, perhaps it won't be as excruciating when it does. I can't live through it again. Richard you are the biggest shit that ever walked the Earth. I hope that new wife of yours screws the entire Mexican army while you're on your honeymoon; and gives you the biggest contagious disease known to man. You deserve that for the way you treated me, you crumb.

It felt good to finally feel something besides pain, she thought as she opened her eyes and looked around. It was then she saw David Levi walking toward the café. He was wearing tan slacks and a black v-neck sweater over a dark plaid sport shirt.

Oh, David, you have come into my life just when I needed you. She smiled to herself and began to raise her hand in a wave. Then she froze with her hand barely off the table.

David removed his dark glasses as he took a seat a few tables across from her. For the briefest of seconds, he looked at her. And, then he looked through her as if she were not even there. For that tiny fraction of a moment, the look in his eyes told Connie all she needed to know. He was here for the Mossad. Do not under any circumstances call attention to him.

To act as natural as she could, she finished looking at him like she would have looked at any other handsome man. Then she casually glanced at some of the other people in the café, hoping if anyone saw her, they would think she was just another young woman in Paris looking for romance. Thankfully, the waiter came with her food so she would have something to do.

But, holy cow, she thought as she picked up her fork. This is as close as I'll ever come to actual intrigue. And, I am sitting across from a Mossad pro. Let's see if I can spot his contact she thought as she laid down her fork and picked up her cup of coffee. She glanced over the rim at the scene before her.

David had leaned back in his chair and was opening the latest edition of *Le Guardian*. Two old French ladies were sitting at the table next to him. Were they his contacts? If they were, Connie knew just what she was going to do when she hit retirement – become an agent. Nope, they got up and left. They hadn't even come near him nor left anything behind on the table. Okay, so much for retirement.

She began to search the other faces of those sitting around her. And, then she froze at whom she saw. She tried to remain calm, but her hands were shaking so badly her cup rattled when she tried to set it back down. Two tables away on her left sat a man from the KGB! He was sitting near the door to the inside of the café. He had his back to the wall and wasn't paying any attention to David at all. He was scanning the people walking by.

The contact wasn't here – someone was coming to meet David. Did he even know the Russians had been tipped off about this meeting? Two weeks ago, Tom had received a dossier concerning this creep. What was his name? It wouldn't come to her, but she did remember he was really bad. His dossier had read like a chapter in Who's Who of Psychotics. Ivan! That's it. Tom and Jeff Evans had dubbed him "Ivan the Weird". Oh, David do you even know he's here?

Frantically, she began to search the crowd walking by. That's when she spotted the woman coming across the boulevard. It had to be the one David was meeting. There was terror on her face. She kept touching her handbag as if checking to make sure something was in there. The woman kept looking around nervously.

Don't do that, lady! Act natural! Connie wanted to scream at her. She glanced back at the KGB man. He hadn't seen the woman yet. He was looking a little to the right of where she was standing on the island waiting to cross the street. Connie looked back at David. He was sitting sideways from the approaching woman, but Connie could see that without turning his face his eyes were riveted on the woman.

David doesn't know. He doesn't know this butcher is less than twenty feet away from him. I've got to do something. I've got to warn him before it's too late. And, I've got to stop Ivan the Weird before he gets a bead on the woman just like I did.

She got up with her cup of coffee and started to walk toward the door of the café in the direction of the table where the Russian was sitting. When she was between the Russian and his line of vision to David and the woman, she tripped and dropped the cup, saucer, and spoon on the Russian's table. Some of the coffee splashed on his suit coat.

"Oh, mah lored!" Connie said as she slapped her hand to her cheek. "What have ah done, Sugar? Ah am sooo soreee, Lover. Ah don't know what came over little ole meee?" Connie crooned and batted her eyelashes at the Russian. She didn't dare meet his murderous stare.

"Don't kill me. Don't kill me. We're in a public place," she prayed silently.

"Why, ah am sooo ashamed of mahself. Here now, let me help you clean that right up, Honey."

"Go away, bitch," the man hissed at her in Russian.

"Why goodness what a pity. You can't even understand me and mah apology. Was that Fa-rench you were speaking, Sugar?"

By this time the waiter had come over and the people sitting in the café were completely absorbed by the spectacle that was going on. As the Russian tried to rise, the waiter began to wipe the coffee off the man's jacket. The Russian pushed his hand away angrily as he tried to see David over the waiter's head.

Good, good. One more delay, thought Connie.

"Why ah have neva done anything lahk this in mah entire life. Wait until I tell everyone back in Georgia that ah spilled coffee on a Fa-renchman. Oh, mah lored! Ah just came to get anotha cup of coffee, because this one got cold and before y'all knew it, ah tripped."

"Please, Mademoiselle, sit down. Sit down, and I will bring you another cup of coffee," the harried waiter said as he wiped up the remains of Connie's coffee on the table. He hurried into the café – as if he were glad to be away from that angry foreign man.

I hoped this worked, David. Because, I just made a complete fool of myself, Connie thought as she walked back to her table with as much dignity as she could.

She checked the island in the middle of the street. The woman was gone. She looked over at David's table. He was still there! He was standing next to the table lighting a cigarette. He blew out the match, tossed it into the ashtray, turned without looking at her or the Russian, and slowly sauntered down the street.

You are one cool son of a gun, David Levi, Connie thought admiringly.

That night the porter at her hotel delivered a dozen long stemmed roses to her room. The card wasn't signed. It simply said, "I owe you one, Sugar".

CHAPTER 21

Two days after the original meet at the café had been aborted, David was having breakfast in his Paris apartment. He was there on assignment for the Mossad. They were running a Soviet spy ring through Paris. The French *Direction Centrale du Renseignement Intérieur* was the most lax of the European spy organizations, so the Mossad based this particular operation in France. David became a part of it two weeks ago.

He looked out the small kitchen window as he thought about what happened at the café. What were the odds he would meet Connie again. He smiled as he remembered the sheer panic he felt when he saw her sitting there. But, she knew what he was doing within seconds and played right along. Because of Connie, a woman's life was saved.

She gave me a chance to warn her off. Of course, the woman was terrified when we met later at the alternative meeting place. I doubt she will work for us again, but the important thing is she is still alive.

Why do I keep running into this crazy, beautiful, American? Is it fate? So far I have been given two major assignments and both times Connie was involved and did something to make me look good. I had no idea the guy sitting at the other table was KGB. We had no information on him at all. Yet she knew he was there. He laughed aloud as he thought about how she called attention to him with the horrible American accent. He shook his head as he smiled.

He stopped as he buttered his toast. "I would like her in my life," he whispered. "She is the one I want to come home to at night and share my day." But, that's not going to happen in this line of work, he thought sadly.

The roads in life we go down lead us to choices. I would never have joined the Mossad if my family hadn't been killed. I would now be a farmer in the desert. But, if I were a farmer, then I never would have met Connie. It was the Mossad road taken that made our lives touch. And, it is the Mossad road that will keep us apart. He laid his knife down and stared across the room at the wall.

The noise of the morning traffic outside his apartment broke his reverie. He took a bite of his toast and dropped the rest back on the plate. Get these thoughts out of your head, Levi, he thought as he brought his dishes to the sink. Time to go to work.

When he arrived at his office, there was a message sitting on his desk to call Aaron. David saw the time was 6:30 a.m. this morning when the message had been received. That meant the call was placed at 5:30 a.m. from Tel Aviv. Jeez, does the man ever sleep? I bet the Temple in Jerusalem he knows about Connie's help on this assignment. He gave a soft laugh as he dialed the familiar number in Israel.

"Shalom."

"Shalom, Aaron. It's me David Levi returning your phone call."

"Ah, David. I just wanted to say *Mozel Tov* on your first operation in Paris. Well, done," Aaron said smoothly.

That old rascal knows. I know he knows. He wouldn't get up at five-thirty this morning just to say "Mozel Tov".

"Thank you Aaron." Then David remained silent. I am going to wait you out, he thought. I can play this game too.

"By the way, I see in your report that you had to abort the original meeting and change to the alternative place, because, let's see . . . " Papers began to rustle on the other end. "Ah, here it is, because of a KGB agent who was sitting in the café when you arrived. His name was Ivan Dobinsky you said. Is that right?"

"Yes, that was his name. At least I think that was his name. I followed him back to his hotel and it was the name he was registered under." David waited for the rest of the questions to come.

"I see. Well, I just have a few minor questions. For example, how is it you knew this man was a KGB agent to begin with? And, not only that, but you even knew he had to be followed. So brilliant on your part."

"The reason I ask," Aaron said with silky bonhomie, "is we have no record of this Russian agent in our files. When we contacted our counterparts in MI-6, they said they had only learned about him two weeks ago. In fact, the only other agency they shared this information with was the CIA. So, how did you, dear boy, know these things?"

Right on target, you sly fox. "Yeah, about that," David said slowly. "Aaron, you are not going to believe what happened."

"Humor me, David."

"It's interesting you use the word humor, Aaron, because what I'm going to tell you does contain a lot of humor."

Then David told Aaron everything – from spotting Connie O'Rourke in the café as he sat down, to spilled coffee and the hilarious accent, to aborting the original meet with the contact.

"I can't believe this," Aaron chuckled.

After a short pause, Aaron added, "You know, we should try to recruit this Connie O'Rourke for the Mossad. She seems like someone we could really use."

David took in a quick breathe of air. What if that happened? Then she would be in my life. Fantasy, Levi. All fantasy.

CHAPTER 22

The Handler was leaning against a tree in the small park across the street from the Ministry of the Army. He was dressed in inexpensive casual clothes; black pants, a white shirt open at the neck, and a tweed sport coat. His shoes were scuffed and worn, since no Soviet citizen would have access to shoe polish. He was reading the evening edition of *Pravda* as he waited for Nicholas to leave work for the evening. The Handler was going to follow Nicholas tonight to see if he could find out just whom this girlfriend of his was.

It was time to find out more about her, since he felt she played a part in why Nicholas told him he was done supplying information for us. As he was waiting, he thought back to his last meeting with Nicholas.

Nicholas called for a meeting with him last Sunday morning at a Russian market close to his Mother's house. The Handler was impressed with Nicholas' choice. The market was away from the central city and wasn't near any secret Soviet installations, therefore, no reason to have this place under watch. He got there early, and smiled when he saw Nicholas already standing at a vegetable stall. He had arrived early also.

You are learning, my friend, he thought as he approached him. They each made a purchase of potatoes, then, walked in the direction of a small tavern down the street. As they walked they made casual conversation. Once inside the tavern, each ordered a shot of vodka, downed it and walked outside again.

Here in the Soviet Union, small taverns could not afford tables and chairs. One drank standing up at the bar. At this time of day, the tavern was crowded with the men who were waiting for their wives to finish shopping at the market. So any talking inside the tavern would be impossible. Once they were away from it, they were able to become serious.

"So, why did you call for this meeting? What do you want to talk to me about, Nicholas?" The Handler asked quietly as the strolled down the street.

"I'm quitting," said Nicholas. "I'm done supplying information to you. I've done all I can and now I want my life back. Setting up my step-father for treason is no longer important to me."

"I thought I told you. You can't quit. You made the decision to come to us. You can never go back to the life you once knew."

"That's *dreck* and you know it. I can quit and I am quitting as of now. You Americans never had any intention of helping me trap my stepfather as a traitor. You just wanted as much information as I could supply; and, you would say anything to get it."

The Handler's mind was racing as he tried to get control of the situation. He knew threats wouldn't work this time. Something major had happened. He needed to find out what it was that changed Nicholas from a scared, complacent follower into this.

"All right, let's calm down a minute and just talk," The Handler said as he turned and looked directly at Nicholas. Nicholas just curled his lip and looked away.

"First, we are not lying to you about wanting to help you set your stepfather up for treason. We want that to happen as much as you do. It would be an enormous coup for us. But, bringing it about and making sure all the pieces fit, takes time. It can't be done overnight. You are not acting like the same person I met and spoke to at your Mother's house two months ago. So now, tell me. What is it? What has changed your mind? Do you want to leave the Soviet Union? Do you want money? Come on Nicholas talk to me, maybe I can help you."

Nicholas wiped a hand over his face. "I . . . I just want my life to be normal again. It's that simple. There is nothing I want from you except to be left alone. This meeting is over. Don't contact me again." Nicholas turned the corner and walked away.

And, that was the end of the conversation last Sunday. The Handler stuffed the newspaper into the pocket of his suit jacket when he saw Nicholas exit the Army building. He began to walk down the sidewalk on the opposite side of the street from him. The Handler slowed his pace keeping him in view. If it wasn't the girlfriend, he thought, then he would continue to have Nicholas put under surveillance until he found out exactly why he wanted to stop. He hoped the answer wasn't because the Soviets were on to him. That could only end in death.

He watched as Nicholas met up with a blond haired woman. She seemed to fit the description of the woman Nicholas met in Gorky Park three weeks ago. He was now a little over a block behind Nicholas and the woman. He couldn't see her face. Six blocks later, he watched as they entered the Moscow Operetta Theatre. He sprinted across the street and was lucky enough to get a ticket in the side box seats.

One good thing about the Soviet Union, they believed in culture. Every day of the week, the people could attend operas, concerts or the ballet somewhere in Moscow. And, the government made sure the ticket prices were affordable, so all the people could enjoy the arts. This country was such a dichotomy, he thought as he hurried up the steps to his seat. Unbelievable culture. Yet, the Soviets had the second biggest arsenal of nuclear weapons in the world. They sent tens of thousands of people to Siberia while strains of Tchaikovsky floated through the streets as if nothing had happened.

The Handler took his seat in the second balcony. Fortunately, his seat in the box was next to the railing. The program had not started so the lights were still up in the theatre. He leaned over the railing and scanned the crowd. The majority of the men in the crowd were military and wearing their uniforms.

Just great, The Handler fumed. How the hell am I going to spot Gregorivch among all these uniforms? The blond hair of the woman, that's how. Very few Russian people had blond hair. After a few minutes, he saw them walking down the aisle to their seats. But, they were too far away to get a good look at the woman's face. The man and woman seated next to him had a pair of small binoculars. He asked if he could borrow them.

He scanned the area. When Nicholas and the woman came into view, The Handler sucked in his breathe and whispered, "Holy shit," without moving his lips. Anya Kaminsky. So, little Anya, are you the cause of this mess? My, my, what a small world, he thought as he smiled internally. He handed the binoculars back to the couple; thanked them; then sat back to enjoy the operetta as the Overture began.

CHAPTER 23

Connie had returned from Paris late yesterday afternoon and was now in Tom's office going over the list of tasks that had to be completed before they left for Moscow next Sunday. It was difficult to come into work today. The gossip about Richard's wedding had died down somewhat while she was gone. The entire office did not come to her desk to tell her about the wedding. But, just being here brought back the pain she was trying so hard to forget. Thank god, no one knew she and Richard had been seeing each other. It would be unbearable if they had.

"That's about it, Connie. I think we have things under control for our move," Tom said as he checked off the last item on their to-do list. He looked at Connie and raised his eyebrows. "So, how are you?"

"Better than the last time you saw me," Connie said as she gave him a weak smile.

"I, ah . . . Look, I'm not really good at this talking thing, Connie. I hope you know I do care about you and worry about you. If, um, you really need to talk to someone about what happened, you can always call Jennie. She's good at that sort of thing."

Connie gave a short laugh. "That's okay, Tom. I'm a private person; and, I need to work through this by myself. But, thank you, anyway."

Tom looked relieved. "How was Paris? You know, I worked there for a short time during the War. I really liked the city."

"Actually, I did enjoy Paris too. And, I want to thank you again for suggesting I go there. It was what I needed to do." A wary look returned to Tom's face. Connie said, "Don't worry, I'm not going to burst into tears and cry on your shoulder. Besides, the crying is over." She stood up and walked to the door. When she had her hand on the doorknob, she hesitated.

Turning back to Tom, she said "By the way, I met two old friends while I was in Paris." She hadn't planned on telling Tom so soon about the meeting in the café. She wanted to get all the details for their move to Moscow finished before she said anything.

"I ran into David Levi and, ah, Ivan Dobinsky," she cocked her head and waited.

"What? Ivan Dobinsky, that butcher! And, wasn't the other guy, the Mossad guy? What the hell happened?" Tom yelled.

"No need to worry, Tom. I'll just call your wife and talk this over with her. Like you said, Jennie's better at this talking thing anyway." Her smile got broader as she watched Tom shoot out of his chair.

"Like hell you will. You get back here and sit down. Holy cow, Connie, you're just a secretary and within months you got yourself involved in some serious espionage. Twice, damn it. Now what the hell happened this time?"

"Just a secretary?" Connie glared at Tom with her hand still on the doorknob.

"Aw, come on, kiddo. You know what I meant. You're not an agent. Now, spill it. How did this meeting come about," Tom said as he began to calm down. He pointed to the chair across from his desk and sat down.

Connie returned to the chair. She told Tom about her chance meeting with David Levi in the cafe; spotting the KGB; spilling the coffee and receiving the roses. "And, that's it. Pretty good for a little ole secretary?" she added with a phony Southern drawl.

"Yeah, it is good for a little old secretary. I don't know how you manage to get yourself into these situations." Tom said shaking his head. "But, now I am very concerned about whether the KGB knows who you are or not. If this Mossad guy can trace you to your hotel room, so can the KGB. We don't want to be hassled when we get to Moscow."

"Oh my God, Tom. I never thought about that."

"This one, I have to report, Connie. Don't worry," Tom added as he saw the alarm on her face. "This doesn't mean you are going to be vetted. But, you will be asked to provide a statement about this. So, you might as well start to write it out when you get back to your desk. Let me see it before you hand it in. We'll try to put a spin on how you already knew the guy from the Mossad."

"Actually," Tom started to smile, "this report should give everyone a good laugh. Even though it was serious with the Russian idiot involved, your quick thinking with the coffee and the bogus accent should be a first for the CIA."

As Connie was leaving again, she turned and looked at Tom. "You know, Tom. I would make a very good spy."

"Not in this lifetime, Connie. No way will I put you in harm's way."

She squinted her eyes and gave him one last look before she raised her chin and walked out the door.

CHAPTER 24

The move to Moscow had gone smoothly. Within two days, Tom Bursak and his team were settled in. Tonight was Tom's first Embassy party being hosted by the French Embassy. The party was in honor of the anniversary of the Soviet launching of Sputnik.

Honor, my ass, Tom fumed as he was standing next to the bar. It still rankled him that the Soviets were the first to put a satellite into orbit. And then, if that wasn't enough, they beat us by putting a manned spacecraft into space right before we did. Well, we'll be sure to wave to them when we land on the moon. He smiled internally as he reached for a glass of wine.

When he turned, he spotted Mislav Boginin, his old nemesis, walking toward him. Years ago, they were field agents together, but on opposite sides.

Today Mislav was the second in command at the KGB. As they met, they began speaking in Russian.

"Mislav, nice to see you again. How are you?" Tom asked.

Mislav raised his glass. "Well, Mr. Bursak, it has been a long time. What brings you to the Soviet Union, my friend? Surely, there is nothing of interest here for the CIA."

Tom looked at Mislav in surprise. "Why Mislav, haven't you heard? I am no longer with the CIA. I'm with the State Department now. I am the new Cultural Attache at the U.S. Embassy."

Mislav gave a crooked smile and squinted his eyes as he looked at Tom who continued to maintain the look of innocence. "Aah, I see. Cultural Attaché," he said nodding his head. Most espionage heads were assigned the title of Cultural Attaché at their Embassies.

The two remained quiet for a moment – each lost in their memories of the past.

"I am a grandfather now, Tom. My son Anton has two children. What about you? How many grandchildren do you have?" Mislav asked.

"None. Neither of my children is married. My wife and I keep hoping though. It seems their jobs are more important to them right now. My son is an officer in the Marines serving at the Pentagon. And, my daughter works at the United Nations in New York. And, Anton, what does he do?"

Mislav shook his head as he smiled. "He is in the government, a member of our Parliament, the *Duma*, if you can believe that. Last week he had the affront to tell me, the KGB was spending too much money. Imagine, my only child a bureaucrat – the very people who gave us such headaches when we were in the field."

He turned to Tom with a serious face. "You know, Tom. I never got the chance back in '48 to contact you personally and thank you. If it hadn't been for you, Anton would have died. I wouldn't be a grandfather now. I do thank you for getting that penicillin across the border to us when he was so sick. The drug saved his life, my friend. My wife thinks you should be Prime Minister."

Tom pursed his lips together and looked down. "Yeah . . . well . . . just because you and I had different jobs to do, didn't mean our children had to suffer for it, Mislav."

He remembered sneaking into the supply unit of the military hospital in Germany to get the penicillin after he learned Mislav's son had pneumonia and was dying. That was the easy part. The hard part was arranging a meeting with the Soviet agent in Berlin who then refused to take the antibiotic back across the border to Mislav. The agent thought Tom was giving him poison and refused to pass it on. He finally agreed when Tom told him it wasn't the agent's decision to make. His job was to get it to Mislav and let Mislav decide whether to administer it to his son.

"Well, Comrade, it was nice to see you again. But, now I must mingle with the other guests here tonight. I suppose your duties as the, ah, Cultural Attaché will bring us together again sometime soon." Mislav raised an eyebrow and chuckled.

"Until then," Tom said as he raised his champagne glass to Boginin.

As Mislav was leaving, Tom's wife, Jennie returned from the powder room. "Who was that man you were speaking to, Tom? It seemed like you two know each other."

"We do. We were opposing field agents in Germany shortly after the War. That's Mislav Boginin. He's the second in command at the KGB now. I like him, but I wouldn't trust him for a second," he said as he watched Mislav approach the Ambassador from France.

"Oh, I see Connie finally arrived," Jennie smiled as she looked across the large room at Tom's secretary who was coming their way. Tom turned and saw her. He lifted his chin and gave her a quick nod.

When Connie had entered the enormous hall she looked around for her boss and his wife; and, finally spotted them across the room standing near the bar area. She smiled and waved at Jennie as she began to walk toward them. When she skirted around a group of people, two, old, Russian officers standing next to the wall ogled her as she past them. They said something in Russian to each other and began to snicker. They went back to drinking their vodkas and didn't notice as Connie's head snapped up and she glared at them. When she turned back and continued walking, her jaw was in a locked position and her eyes were tiny slits. With her head down and her shoulders forward, she marched toward Tom and Jennie who were both smiling in anticipation.

"Oh, oh, Tom. Something just happened when she walked past those two Russian military men.

See that look she just gave them? This is priceless. I can't wait to find out what just happened," Jennie looked back at Tom with a big grin on her face.

"Oh, brother," groaned Tom. "One of these days she's going to start World War III with those blatant looks of hers."

Without even saying hello, Connie began her tirade. "Do you know what those two old farts said about me? The fat one said he would like to grab my ass. And, the other, old beanpole said he would like to squeeze my tits!" she looked back at them with pure fury.

"Well, you know what? I'm going back there and tell that fat dwarf he has a little pecker. Then, I'm going to tell the other one he couldn't get laid if he paid for it. And, I am going to do it in Russian too."

"Easy, Connie," Tom said as Jennie laughed uproariously.

"And, I know how to say those words in Russian too, Tom. One night our Russian study group got our professor drunk and made him to tell us how to say all the naughty words in Russian. We took notes . . . too bad they weren't on the exam, we would have all gotten an A."

"Come on, kiddo. Calm down. I thought we agreed to keep the fact you speak Russian quiet while we were here.

Later in the evening as Tom was speaking to the Cultural Attaché from the British Embassy, he spotted Igor Polakova enter the room with a beautiful, young woman on his arm.

That has got to be Polakova's mistress, Tom thought. Russian wives of middle-aged men do not look like that. He's got balls bringing her here.

"Whose the woman with Polakova?" Tom asked his British counterpart.

"The one with the healthy looking chest?" the attaché asked as he looked sideways at Tom and smirked. "That's his mistress. Word has it, she has a lot of power over him," he answered.

"She must have in order for him to be so blatant bringing her to an Embassy party," Tom added. "Seems the army men have all the luck." It was Tom's turn to look sideways and smirk.

As the attaché walked away, Tom looked for Jennie. She was across the room talking to Connie and another woman from the Danish Embassy. He was just going to join her when he saw Nicholas Gregorovich and a blond woman walking toward the bar. Their path was going to take them directly along side of Connie.

Oh, no, Tom thought frantically. There is no way Connie will be able to keep a straight face when she spots him. So help me, if she gives him away, I'll kill her.

Just then Connie turned and bumped right into Gregorovich. Tom watched helpless as Connie grabbed him to steady herself. She smiled and said something to him. For the briefest of seconds, recognition played across her face and then nothing but another smile and a nod. Gregorovich said something to Connie and nodded. Then he took the blond woman's elbow and continued on to the bar. Connie turned back to Jennie and the other woman as if nothing had happened. But, as she was talking with them, she looked at Gregorovich and the woman out of the corner of her eye.

Tom took in a deep breath and let it out. I think I just had a heart attack, he thought. I was sure Connie would have blown it the minute she realized who Gregorovich was. But, she didn't. When the hell did she learn to keep such important emotions in check? He looked around the room for Mislav Boginin to see if he had seen the exchange. Mislav had his back to them and apparently saw nothing. Thank god for that. Without hurrying, he began to cross the room to Jennie.

Later, when he had a chance to get Connie alone, he said quietly, "You did an excellent job of not showing recognition when you bumped into Gregorovich. I always know what you're thinking. I thought for sure you would give him away. But, you didn't. Nice job, kiddo."

"You underestimate me, Tom," Connie said. "I know when to be a professional." Connie looked around the room acting like this was a mere conversation between the two of them. "Besides," Connie added looking at her glass of wine, "as far as Gregorovich is concerned, he doesn't even know I exist."

"What do you mean, he doesn't know you exist?"

"Oh, Tom. Sometimes you can be so dense," Connie said as she looked up at Tom. "I watched him. The way he looked at the woman he's with. It was so plain. He is in love with her. I could have fallen at his feet and he wouldn't have noticed me."

"What?" Tom asked dumbfounded. As far as he knew, there was no mention of a woman in the picture. First thing tomorrow, he would meet with Gregorovich's handler. Time to get up to speed here, he thought.

Mislav Boginin did not see Connie bump into Nicholas, but Igor Polakova did.

He was standing on the opposite side of the room with a frown on his face. Why did that woman bump into Nicholas? She looks American. He needed to find out who she was. This might be a way to finally get rid of his stepson whom he loathed. The contact following Nicholas was proving useless. Perhaps, he could get rid of Nicholas the same way he got rid of his father – simply with innuendo. Igor smiled as he thought about this. Maybe it was time to talk to Mislav Boginin, that oily bastard.

CHAPTER 25

The next morning at the U.S. Embassy, Tom was reviewing the file on Nicholas Gregorovich when his phone rang. It was Connie on the inter-office line.

"Tom, your nine o'clock appointment is here," Connie said.

"Thanks. Send him in."

Nicholas's handler entered the room and closed the door behind him. This was the first time they met. Tom rose and offered his hand.

"Sit down, Joe. It's nice to finally meet you," Tom said as he smiled.

"Thanks," Joe said with little inflection in his voice as he nodded and took a seat across from Tom.

"I've been reading your reports for a number of years now, Joe. Very well done. I want to go over a few things in the Gregorovich file." Tom looked up from the file and was startled to see the distain on Joe's face. Then he smiled to himself. The son-of-a-bitch is sitting here thinking he's talking to a Washington bureaucrat. Don't blame him. At one time, I would have done the same thing. Okay, time to let him know I wrote the book on fieldwork.

"Perhaps, I should start by introducing myself," Tom began all the while looking into Joe's eyes. "I began working for the O.S.S. shortly after the War. Once the war was over, we knew our next biggest problem was going to be the Russians. I ran over two hundred operations in almost all of the countries behind the Iron Curtain. The only country I never got to was Romania. At one time, I had fifty-three agents under me. Do you still do the newspaper left on the table drop? I invented that one."

He watched as realization struck and Joe began to smile and shake his head. "I apologize, Tom. You have to understand my point of view. You're only going to be here for the interim. Because of that, I just assumed you were some pain-in-the-ass desk jockey filling in until a permanent man could be appointed."

Then he added, "With your background, you know how arrogant we field agents can be. Again, I'm sorry."

"No problem," Tom said happy to have set the record straight. "Can we talk about Nicholas Gregorovich now?"

"Sure. What do you need to know about him," Joe replied still looking sheepish.

"Why has he stopped working with us? We can't let someone who can lead us directly to Polakova just walk away. What happened?" Tom asked.

"Well, that's just it. He won't tell us what it is that is making him stop. I met with him ten days ago when he dropped the bomb. I thought I would let him calm down a bit before I go back. I don't think the Russians are on to him. I don't get the feeling that's the reason. If it were, it seems to me, he would be begging us to get him out of the country. And, he's not."

Tom scratched his head. "You know, last night, I was at a party at the French Embassy. While there, my secretary literally bumped into Gregorovich. Later, she said something interesting. I've been with her long enough to know when to pay attention to things seen through her eyes. She said Gregorovich didn't even know she existed, because he was so in love with the blond woman he was with. This morning, I pulled out his file and learned he has recently been seen numerous time with a blond woman."

Joe reached for a pack of cigarettes from his shirt pocket. Then he patted his pants pockets as he tried to locate his lighter.

Tom slid his desk lighter toward Joe. "According to the file, we have very little information about her. But, we do know the woman's name is Anya Kaminsky. Interesting last name, don't you think?"

"Ah . . . well . . . Kaminsky is like Smith here. Many people have that last name in Russia," Joe replied as he lit his cigarette.

Tom raised his eyebrows and shrugged his shoulders as he looked at Joe. "Isn't it interesting that you have the same last name, Joe?" Tom waited as Joe took a drag on his cigarette and blew the smoke out slowly.

Joe looked at Tom, shook his head, and pursed his lips together. "She's my cousin, he said quietly as he looked down at his hands. "Our fathers were brothers. And, what's worse, she lives with her grandmother."

"You haven't told her, have you?"

"Of course, not." Joe's head jerked up as he raised his voice. "I would never put her life in danger by contacting her. I would never do that to any innocent person." He glared at Tom.

After a moment, he added quietly again, "You know what a shock it was when I discovered Gregorovich's girl friend was my cousin? Her grandmother is my grandmother. And, I can't tell either of them who I am, because of this job. The same goes for my father. He thinks I'm here working for the State Department. He showed me old photos of his mother before I came here and asked me to try to find her. He wants to know if she is even alive." Joe shook his head. "Do you know how hard it is to do nothing? Some days this job stinks, Tom."

Tom sat with his elbows on the desk and his chin resting on his folded hands. He said, "I know. I know how hard this job can be at times." He spread his hands out in a useless gesture. After a moment, he blew out a breath of air.

"Joe, we can't let this drop. We've got to get Gregorovich back working for us. Bringing Polakova down is just too important. Now that we know your cousin is close to Gregorovich, we need to plan this very carefully. We can't let her be hurt from the fall out. I'll clear my calendar for every morning at nine. Let's plan on meeting every day until we come up with something that will speed things up. Something that will work and at the same time keep those three people as safe as we can."

CHAPTER 26

Igor Polakova was in a pensive mood. He sat at his desk with his chair turned toward the windows. It was raining. He watched as the rain ran down the windows in filthy streaks. They were so dirty, even the rain couldn't make them clean. The lights were on in his office, but the gloom of the day and the grime on the windows made the interior of his office dreary. All these workers here in the Soviet Union, he thought, and we never think of having them do something as simple as cleaning windows.

He turned back to his desk. It was time to review his plan to get rid of Nicholas. He had waited long enough. However, he still had two weeks before he could even begin to put his plan into place. Nicholas was currently on tour of the Eastern Front military installations to assess their response readiness.

As Igor saw it, the biggest problem wouldn't be setting Nicholas up for the fall. His biggest problem was going to be working with that KGB pig, Mislav Boginin. The plan had to be airtight or Mislav would pounce like a rat on garbage. If he even thought something was not right, he would widen his net to include me. It was uncanny how Mislav's mind worked. Just the thought of it made him shudder. Nicholas was the one who was going to spend the rest of his life in the Gulag, not him.

He planned to order Nicholas to prepare a paper on the entire Soviet nuclear capabilities on the pretext it would be presented to an elite group of military generals. The paper was to be highly classified. He was to tell no one what he was working on. Igor would give him the official documentation to allow Nicholas to enter the secret vaults where the nuclear information was stored. Those same official papers would allow him to copy and then remove whatever copied documents were necessary to prepare the paper. However, Igor planned to have his mistress sign Igor's name on the admittance papers.

After Nicholas went into the vaults and retrieved the secret documents, Igor would contact Boginin with his concerns that he felt Nicholas had been acting odd and could possibly be stealing nuclear secrets. Boginin would find the nuclear documents in Nicholas possession and when he checked the signature on the admittance papers, he would discover Igor's signature had been forged. He, of course, would deny he ever signed such a document or that he ever told Nicholas to prepare any such paper.

And, he would be sure to bring up the name of that woman at the American Embassy who bumped into Nicholas at the French Embassy the other night. Nothing positive, just a vague innuendo. Implicating the Americans in espionage never hurt.

He doubted there would even be a trial. It would be too embarrassing for the Soviet Union to admit something like this to the rest of the world. No, the KGB would probably solve the problem by quietly killing Nicholas and be done with it. Igor smiled at this last thought.

He also needed to make a phone call to the agent watching Nicholas. It was time to call the agent off and away from Nicholas.

CHAPTER 27

Nicholas was sitting in a bar in the Old Town section in Riga, Latvia. He was with his friend, Andre who was on this assignment with him representing the Eastern Front Military Supply Unit. This was no picnic being here. Both he and Andre were wearing long underwear, wool sweaters, wool pants and wool knit socks inside their boots, The cold, moist winds off the Baltic Sea in late autumn seemed to seep into one's soul. Bone chilling was a good description – the cold went deep into the bones. One could never get warm here. Even inside the buildings the cold clung to the walls and furniture.

The Soviets built huge central heating plants in the cities of all the countries they occupied, which did nothing to ward off the cold. The reason for the lack of heat was the Soviets either ran the heating pipes loosely wrapped in insulation above the ground where the heat quickly vanished or laid the pipes so shallow in the ground, the heat was quickly absorbed. Latvia was no exception. By the time the heat from the plants arrived at the buildings, it was nothing but cold.

At least the pre-Soviet buildings, built with thick stone and mortar, had a better chance of being somewhat warm. But not the Soviet built apartment and office buildings. In order to contain the masses, the Soviets not only built the central heating plants, but they constructed thousands upon thousands of poor, cheap, shoddy apartment and office build-ings in every single city in every country. So, even if some heat did reach those buildings, it was lost through the poorly insulated walls and cheap win-dows.

Sitting in the bar in the cold in Latvia, he and Andre were discussing the ballet, of all things. The discussion began when Andre asked if Nicholas had seen the new kid from Riga, Mikhail Baryshnikov, who was dancing with the Kirov Ballet in Leningrad. Andre had seen him when the Kirov came to Moscow.

"He is going to be better than Nureyev someday," said Andre. "Nicholas do you know that Rudolf

Nureyev didn't die like they told us in the newspaper? The son-of-a-bitch defected in 1961 and is alive and well and dancing in Paris now."

"You're out of your mind, Andre. Where did you hear that drivel?"

"It's true. One of my comrades came back from East Berlin last year. He said he heard it on *Radio Free Europe* – you know that radio station the Americans bombard us with."

"Oh, come on Andre. That's just Western propaganda. I don't believe it."

Andre was drinking directly out of his second bottle of vodka. He had given up using a shot glass half way through the first one. He kept the bottle in his hand and used it for emphasis.

"You know, Nicholas, you've changed. You seem calmer, not so angry anymore. What is it? Is Anya having that much effect on you?"

Nicholas was surprised at Andre's comment. He wasn't aware his hatred of Igor had been so obvious. And, maybe it was Anya more than his decision not to work with the Americans anymore that was making him calm.

"Love makes you mellow, Andre. You should try it," he replied.

Andre just sneered. "You have changed, my friend; but you are still so naïve, Nicholas. There is no such thing as love here in the Soviet Union. Everyone looks out only for himself and trusts no one. That's how we survive. Not on love."

"Andre, Andre. Keep your voice down, my friend," hissed Nicholas. He stood up then and took his friend by the arm. "Come on. I'll take you back to the barracks," he whispered and helped Andre into his coat.

Once outside they began weaving their way toward the Army barracks located on the other side of Old Town. Andre was so drunk and unsteady on his feet that Nicholas had to brace himself with his arm around Andre to keep them both from falling on the icy cobblestones.

Andre turned toward Nicholas and patted him clumsily on his chest as he whispered in his face, "Nicholas. Let's defect," he slurred. He tried to push Nicholas toward the Daugava River. "Come on. Let's steal a boat and row down the Daugava out to the Baltic. Then on to Sweden," he giggled. "How far can it be? Three or four hundred kilometers? We can be there by morning."

"You need to sleep this off, Andre," Nicholas said finding it more difficult to keep his friend steady.

"I only hope you pass out before we reach the barracks so no one else hears what you are saying, you crazy fool."

As they neared the barracks, Nicholas was now struggling to keep Andre up right. He was holding him with both arms as they reeled toward the gate. He spoke softly in his friend's ear. "Not another word, you drunken idiot. I will kill you myself if you get us in trouble." He needn't have bothered, because just then Andre's eyes rolled up in his head; and, he proceeded to pass out and slide to the ground.

Nicholas had to pay two returning soldiers 10 rubles each to help him carry Andre to their room. The Sentry at the gate had been no help. He wanted to leave Andre lying on the ground. Andre may be right. Soviets are only out for themselves. No one helps anyone here unless they get something for themselves.

After he got Andre settled, he sat on his bed smoking a cigarette. What kind of life is this, he wondered. There isn't a day that goes by, I don't see some drunk passed out on the street. Men, women, it makes no difference. We drink ourselves into oblivion just to survive.

For one brief moment, his heart leaped tonight when Andre suggested they defect. Could he and Anya, for he would not go without her, somehow get out of the Soviet Union? Would it be possible? Of course, she wouldn't go without her grandmother. How do we get her out? Maybe if we vacationed down in Yugoslavia and climbed over the Italian Alps into Italy. Maybe, I should contact the Americans again. I bet they could help us.

Oh, stop it! Stop thinking these crazy thoughts. Get them out of your head, you stupid fool. There is no way out of here.

When he got back to Moscow, he would tell Anya about what happened tonight though. He needed to know what she would think about this.

CHAPTER 28

Tom Bursak wasn't feeling well. As soon as he got out of bed this morning, he felt lousy. It must be the flu, he thought as he rubbed his chest and then rotated his left arm. He and Connie were reviewing the write-up of the notes of his meeting with Joe Kaminsky regarding Nicholas Gregorovich.

Connie was scanning her copy. "Tom, this is something. Nicholas' girlfriend is really Joe's cousin? What are the odds of that happening? This certainly complicates things, doesn't it?"

Sweat formed on his brow. Why was it so hot in here, Tom thought as he loosened his tie? He was having trouble focusing on what Connie was saying.

"How do you want me to transmit these notes to Washington?" she asked as she looked up at her boss.

"Tom, what's wrong? You don't look well. I'm calling the Embassy nurse." Connie reached for the phone on Tom's desk and began dialing the internal number.

"Someone answer the phone," Connie said as it was ringing. Tom was looking worse by the second.

"We need medical help right now," Connie shouted when the person answered. "Room 214. Something is very wrong with my boss."

Why was there such pain in his chest? It felt like an elephant was sitting on him. Panic set in. Heart attack. I'm having a heart attack, he thought wildly.

No! Not now. Not here. Jennie. The kids. He looked at Connie with sheer terror on his face. He pushed himself away from the desk and tried to stand. For some reason that seemed important to him.

I need to tell her something. He was trying to get the words out as he grabbed his chest. He heard screaming. It was so hard to see now. The darkness. If he could only breathe, but the elephant wouldn't let him take a breath.

"Jennie," came out as Tom pitched forward and fell to the floor.

"Tom! On my God, Tom!" Connie ran around the desk and grabbed him just as he slid to the floor.

"Help! Someone help me!" Connie yelled as she turned Tom onto his back. His eyes were open but were no longer capable of focusing.

Connie began CPR as she continued to shout for help. A marine rushed into the room with his gun drawn. It took seconds for him to assess the situation. He came around the desk holstering his gun and knelt down beside her.

"I'll take over, Ma'am," he said moving Connie out of the way.

"Don't you dare, Tom. Don't you dare," Connie kept repeating over and over again as she stood and watched helplessly. "Don't you dare die."

The Embassy nurse arrived and retrieved the defibrillator pads. She tried three times to restart Tom's heart, but it was no use. She bowed her head and said quietly, "It's over. He's dead."

It was cold in Washington for November. But, Connie wasn't even aware of the temperature as she stood beside Tom's grave. The priest was ending his homily at the gravesite. Connie never heard a word he said. She was alone with her thoughts. Her Dad stood next to her holding her hand.

Why you, Tom? Why did you have to die? So many horrible people on this planet, but it was you who died.

I believe when we get to heaven there will be a Why Line where we will get our all of our Earthly questions answered. I am going to be first in line. You can count on it, Tom. Because, I want to know why people like you and my mother had to die when you both had so much left to give.

When the burial service was over, she and her father headed back to their car. Jeff Evans, now the acting head of the Russian desk at the CIA, approached Connie.

"Do you have a minute, Connie? Mr. O'Rourke, would you mind if I talked to your daughter in private?" he asked as he took Connie's arm.

"Of course not," Lee replied. "I'll be waiting in the car for you, Honey."

When they were away from the people leaving the cemetery, Jeff looked at Connie. "This is one of the worst days of my life. Tom and I knew each other for 25 years. We were going to retire at the same time." He looked back at Tom's casket where Jennie and Tom's son and daughter remained.

He shook his head as if to clear it. "I know this is going to sound crass saying this right now. Look, Connie, the DCI would like you to stay on in Moscow for a few months."

"Jeff, I don't think I would be . . . "

"I know this is difficult for you, Connie. But, we need you for the transition."

"Who are you appointing as the new station chief in Moscow, Jeff?"

"We don't know yet. We have several people in mind. But, the ultimate decision rests with the DCI. Please, Connie. Stay and help us."

"All right, I'll stay in Moscow, but, only for two months. Then I want to come home." Tears started running down her cheeks.

CHAPTER 29

Upon returning to Moscow, Connie was working with Joe Kaminsky packing up Tom Bursak's personal belongings. Per protocol, an Embassy, Marine guard was stationed at Tom's office door to monitor the packing. When Connie was wrapping the family picture of Tom and Jennie and their children, she stopped.

"Joe, this is one of the hardest things I ever had to do. When I was at the funeral, I told Jeff Evans I would stay on for two months to help the new station chief get acclimated. But, I don't think I can last that long."

"I can understand how you feel, Connie. I only worked with Tom for a few weeks, but even I am going to miss him. Look, rather than make any decisions, why don't you just go one day at a time?" Joe offered.

"Maybe you're right. My first reaction is to just leave, but no matter where I go, I'll be taking my memories with me. So what difference does it make where I am, right?"

Joe smiled and nodded. "Let's take a break, Connie. Are you hungry? Let's go down to the Embassy cafeteria?"

"Okay, I could use a cup of coffee about now," she said as she put Tom's picture in the box.

"Joe, how do you like working in the Soviet Union?" Connie asked as she reached their table. "Do you ever miss not being able to go home very often?"

"Well truthfully," he said as he put his tray down, "I find Russia fascinating, but that's probably because of my heritage. Both of my parents were born here. The way the Russians think – that pessimistic outlook – and the music, it's in my soul," he smiled as he said this. "How about you? Don't you have a pull to all things Irish, Miss O'Rourke?"

"*Touché,*" Connie smiled back.

"What are you going to do about your grandmother and your cousin, Joe? I know you can't tell them who you are for security reasons. But, will you ever let them know? I think they need meet you, especially your own grandmother. She needs to know that your father is alive and well."

Joe took a sip of his coffee. "If I ever get reassigned, I plan on telling them who I am before I leave, but, not now – not with Anya being Gregorovich's girlfriend. Even he doesn't know my real name, in case he gets caught. One thing I admired about Tom was the fact he understood the seriousness of this job. One wrong move here and people die. Like it or not, those are the rules of the game."

"Well, that's enough of this type of talk, Connie. Come on," he said as he stood up. "We should be able to finish packing this afternoon."

The American Ambassador came in to Tom's office as Connie and Joe were working.

"Hi. I thought you two would like to know who your new boss is going to be. I just received a coded message from Washington," he said as he unfolded the cable. He looked up and asked, "Either of you know Richard Morgan?"

Connie fell back into Tom's chair. The air was knocked out of her. Dear lord, this can't be true, she thought frantically. I can't possibly face him. I've got to leave. I can't stay. What if I can't get out before Richard gets here? Help me!

"Connie, are you okay?" the Ambassador asked looking worried.

Connie gave a weak smile. "Ah, I, I'm fine. I guess I just reacted to someone else filling Tom's place."

"I understand." He looked down at the other envelope he was holding and handed it to Connie. "Oh, by the way, this came for you. I picked it up when I got the coded message about the new Station Chief."

It was a sealed, "eyes only" communication addressed to her. Connie looked at it and did nothing.

"Well, I'll leave you two to your work here," the Ambassador said as he turned and headed for the door.

Joe had been watching everything that had gone on. After the Ambassador shut the door, he unfolded his arms and slowly walked to Tom's desk. He rested his hands on the desk and leaned forward looking at Connie with a slight smile on his lips and his eyes questioning.

"You know who this Richard Morgan is, don't you. And, I'm not going to like the guy, am I?"

Connie lowered her head in her hands. "Probably . . . not," she said softly.

Connie picked up the envelope the Ambassador had given her and left Tom's office. "I'll be back," is all she said as she walked out.

She passed her desk. I have to be alone, she thought as she went into the woman's bathroom. Once inside the stall, she sat down, wrapped her arms around her waist and began rocking back and forth.

"What am I going to do? What am I going to do?" she whispered.

Without even thinking, she began to open the sealed envelope. It took a moment for her eyes to focus on the contents. It was a personal message from the desk of Jeff Evans.

Dear Connie –

Please believe me when I say I did NOT have anything to do with the appointment of Richard as the new Station Chief in Moscow. I would never do that to you.

This was a decision made by the DCI. Apparently, he and Richard's father-in-law are close friends. The DCI did a favor for his friend. We couldn't talk him out of it.

I am sorry about the way this has played out. <u>Please don't leave, Connie</u>. *We need you more than ever to remain in Moscow.*

If you need to communicate with me, do it by courier and "eyes only".

Connie put the message back in the envelope. As she was walking back to Tom's office, she thought, forget you, Jeff. Forget this job. And, forget you, Richard. You snake.

CHAPTER 30

Before he left on his assignment, Nicholas and Anya had agreed to meet at his mother's house when he returned. They were going to spend another weekend together again. Anya was using the excuse of staying at Katrina's apartment for the benefit of her grandmother. Nicholas smiled. I'm sure Anya's grandmother knows exactly what's going on. The old rascal is no fool.

There was a soft knock on the front door. Nicholas couldn't open it fast enough. Standing at the entrance, Anya looked more beautiful each time he saw her. "Anya, my love," he said as he took her in his arms and kissed her.

Anya hastily stepped out of his embrace. "Nicholas, what will your neighbors think? Come let us go inside," she said as she took his hand.

"The neighbors will think how lucky I am to have such a beautiful girlfriend," Nicholas smiled as he closed the door and took her in his arms once again.

Again, Anya quietly slipped out of his arms. "Nicholas, I will not be able to stay for the weekend. My grandmother is not feeling well. I will have to leave tonight."

"What? No, that can't be, Anya. I missed you so much while I was gone. I have much to tell you. What's wrong with your grandmother?"

"She . . . she complained about being dizzy this morning. I don't want to leave her alone for too long. I am sorry, Nicholas. I hope you understand."

"Well, I do not understand. I was looking forward to our being alone for a few days. When do you have to leave? " Nicholas said frowning.

"I said that I would be home by eight o'clock tonight."

He took her hand. "All right. Come. I have tea prepared in the kitchen for us. Let us at least enjoy the little time we do have," Nicholas said as he kissed her on the cheek.

"So, what have you been doing while I have been gone?" he asked as he poured the tea into the cups already set out on the table.

"Things have been quiet while you were away. My grandmother and I went to the Bolshoi Ballet and saw *Swan Lake*. I never get tired of seeing it. Just the music alone is so beautiful."

"That is a coincidence. Andre and I were talking about the ballet when we were in Riga. He told me that Nureyev did not die. Did you know that? He defected to Paris. But, by the time Andre told me this he was pretty drunk. I don't know if I can believe him. Have you ever heard anything about that?"

"Don't be silly. Nureyev died in 1961. We all know that," replied Anya while taking her first sip of tea.

Nicholas put his cup down and reached for Anya's hand. He looked into her eyes as he began.

"I have to tell you what else Andre said. You have to remember he was drunk. In fact, he passed out right in front of the barrack's gate. But, when we were in Riga on our way back from the tavern, Andre said he and I should defect." Nicholas said the last sentence in a whisper.

Tears came to Anya's eyes. She held his hand tighter. "Nicholas, I want you to promise me if you ever have a chance to defect, you will do it."

"Anya I would never go without you. I love you," he said as she began to openly weep. He tried to wipe the tears running down her cheeks. She pulled away and stood up.

"My love. What is wrong?" he asked baffled.

"Nicholas, I love you too. Oh, how I love you. I want you to believe that. The only thing that matters to me is to know you are safe. Please tell me you will defect if you ever get the chance," she pleaded.

"Anya, safe from what, from whom?" he said as he stood and put his arms around her. This time she did not pull away. She put her head on his shoulder and began to sob.

"We cannot . . . we cannot be together anymore, Nicholas," she said between sobs. "I have been told to stop seeing you."

"What? Who told you? Anya, what is going on? Tell me. Please."

She stood in his arms as she got herself under control. She wiped away the tears on her face with both hands. She seemed to have reached a decision. She took a deep breath and let it out.

"Sit down, Nicholas," she said as she returned to her chair. Her voice was calmer now. It had more strength.

"I was assigned to follow you."

"By whom," Nicholas asked bewildered.

"Igor Polakova," she said angrily.

"Igor! How do you even know him?" he roared. "What are you? One of his whores," he added savagely.

"Nicholas, we made love in this house. You know well I never slept with anyone until you. I met him through Katrina. We were introduced to him one night when we were at a café. Katrina went home with him that night, of course. But, the next day, he called me and asked me to meet him for dinner. He told me he needed my help."

"And, I should believe that? You went to dinner hoping to better yourself with the big general. What happened? Too slow for him, so you had to settle for something lower." Nicholas wanted to hurt her with his words. But, Anya did not react to his harsh words.

"I thought it had something to do with my job at the utilities company," she spat right back at him. "But, I was wrong. During dinner he told me he wanted me to meet you and then follow you. He wanted me to report back to him. Nicholas, he told me if I did not do this, he would send my grandmother and me to Siberia. Then, he even hinted he would have my grandmother killed. I . . . had . . . no . . . choice!" she yelled at him.

Minutes passed in silence, then she added. "Then I did meet you. And, I fell in love with you. If you believe nothing, Nicholas, please believe that."

He sneered at her and turned away. "What did you tell him about me?" he asked. Other than that one meeting in Gorky Park, she was never present at any of his other meetings with the Americans.

"Nothing. I never had anything to report. That is why he told me not to see you anymore. Apparently, I am useless to him. Nicholas, I don't know why he wanted you watched. I think, because I could not help Igor, he is planning something else. That's why I told you to go if you have a chance to defect. If I cannot live my life with you, I need to know in my heart you are safe."

He wiped his hand over his face and turned back to Anya with sad eyes. She watched as he rose and went into the living room. He raised the corner of the rug. He picked it up the letter Igor had written to Stalin and held it in his hands. For a few moments he didn't move. He just stared down at the letter. Turning, he went back to the kitchen and laid the letter on the table next to Anya then went to stand at the window with his back to her.

She unfolded the letter and began to read. When he turned around there were tears streaming down her face, but she made no sound.

"I want to stay here tonight with you , Nicholas. We will get through this together."

"You never answered my question, Anya. Would you defect?"

"I don't know," she said as she took his hand and walked toward the bedroom.

CHAPTER 31

Connie walked up the steps of the Embassy. This was Richard's first day here in Moscow. She had decided to stay and face him, the bastard. She spent the last two nights wide-awake most of the night trying to sort out her thoughts. She finally accepted the fact that running away would solve nothing. Chances are at some other time they would meet again – if not here, then in Washington or another posting. That would be worse, to be taken by surprise. So, she decided to stay and get this first meeting over with.

When she reached her desk, she saw Tom's office door was closed. I have to stop calling it *Tom's* office, she thought sadly. Just then the phone on her desk rang. It startled her. It took a moment for Connie to process the fact she had to answer it. It was an internal call. On the third ring, she picked it up.

"Hello."

"Connie, it's Richard. Can you come into my office for a moment?"

"All right."

I think I'm going to be sick to my stomach, she thought as she rose from her desk.

She opened the door and stepped inside. And, there he was.

"Hello, Richard."

"Connie," he smiled. "It's good to see you again."

She said nothing in return. She didn't sit down. She didn't move. Her face showed no emotion. She just looked at him.

After the silence hung in the air, Richard finally spoke again. "Uh, yes, well. I'm wondering if you can bring me up to speed regarding what's going on here in Moscow."

"Of course. I need to get my notes. I'll be right back," she said without any inflection in her voice. She went to her desk and retrieved the things she needed. When she returned, she closed the door and took a seat across from him and then waited.

Richard seemed to be getting the message, because he could no longer look directly at her. He started to straighten things on his desk. He cleared his throat.

"I reviewed as many files as I could before I left Washington. I think I have a good grasp as to what's happening here. But, I would like to hear what you and Tom were working on"

Connie opened the top file and methodically gave Richard a synopsis of all the cases. Occasionally, she handed Richard a document or communication to help clarify an issue. She did all of this without making eye contact.

Oh, this is stupid, Connie thought. We've met. It's over. Don't let him strip you of your dignity yet again.

She looked directly at him. "Those are all the things we were working on. Is there anything else you need to know?"

"No. You've done your usual fantastic job, Connie."

How would you know what type of job I do, you jerk. She began gathering her files.

"Connie, I want you to know it's good to see you again."

"How's your *wife*, Richard?" She didn't mean to say that. It just slipped out. And, she couldn't keep the distain out of her voice.

"Look, Connie, I really liked you. I still do. But, I had to think about my career. I tried several times to get you to be on my side and give me information to help me. But, you were always so loyal to your dear old Tom," he said with a sneer.

"Don't you dare demean Tom," she lashed out. "He had more integrity than you will ever have."

"I plan on being a powerhouse in Washington some day," Richard said smugly. "And, I don't intend to wait until I'm old and senile to do it. It's not what you know, Connie. It's who you know. Once I realized you wouldn't be able to help me accomplish my goal, I had to look for someone who could. Mary Elizabeth and my father-in-law were the ones who could. It's that simple."

She couldn't even answer him. She was so angry.

"How do you think I got this job?" he went on. "Once I knew I wasn't even being considered for this posting, I made a phone call to my father-in-law; and, told him what I wanted," he smirked. "And, Voila. It seems he and the DCI were at Harvard together. Rah, rah. Harvard boys do stick together, you know. I swore one day I would get Tom's job. And, now I have."

There was absolutely nothing she could say to that. So, she merely turned around and walked out the door.

How could I have been so stupid? Connie wanted to scream. *I am better than this. He will not degrade me anymore than he has. I am contacting Jeff and demanding a transfer right now.*

The next night, Connie arrived at the British Embassy party. As she entered the room, she spotted two friends from the Italian Embassy across the room. They were surrounded by a large group of various other Embassy people who were laughing and having a good time. Connie smiled as she went to join them. One thing about the Italians, their Embassy never hosted parties, but they all showed up when the others did. And, they always had a marvelous time while they were there.

Before she could reach her friends, Richard came up to her. She groaned.

"Hello, Connie. I didn't know you would be here tonight."

"There is no reason why I wouldn't be," she said tersely.

"Can I get you something to drink?"

"No." I can't get out of Moscow fast enough, she thought.

"Connie, the man in the grey suit over near the picture of the Queen, that's Mislav Boginin, right? It looks like he is coming over here to speak to me."

Oh, my god, the idiot doesn't even know who his counterpart is. No wonder Jeff wanted me to stay.

"Yes, and you need to be careful of him. Tom said he would never trust him."

"Oh, here we go again. Tom, Tom, Tom. Well, he's not here anymore. I am, Connie. And, I'm sure I know how to handle Boginin."

She was so stunned. She couldn't think of any comeback before Boginin reached them.

"*Dovz vidanya*, Mr. Morgan," Mislav said when he came up to them and reached out his hand to Richard.

"Good evening, Mr. Boginin," Richard answered as he shook his hand.

You jerk, two seconds ago you weren't even sure who he was, Connie seethed.

Richard waved his hand in Connie's general direction. "Oh, and this is my secretary, Connie O'Rourke."

Mislav bowed to Connie and then began speaking in Russian. "*I understand you not speak Russian. What shame. However, I brought interpreter to help us speak together.*"

"I understand you do not speak Russian. However, I have brought an interpreter, so that we may speak to one another," said the interpreter.

"*First, welcome to Soviet Union. We glad always to have people see our glorious country.*"

"I would like to welcome you to the Soviet Union. We are happy always for people to visit our glorious country." The interpreter looked at Richard for reply.

"Thank you. I am happy to be in your country," Richard answered.

"*My condolences on death of Tom Bursak. He was good man. I shall miss him.*"

Mislav looked at Connie as he said this. He nodded his head at her when he finished.

"You have my condolences on the death of Tom Bursak. He was a very good man. And, I personally shall miss him."

"Well, of course. But, that's the way life is, people die," Richard replied.

The minute Richard's answer was interpreted, Mislav's face shut down. He looked at Richard. It took him a moment to continue.

"*Tell me. As Cultural Attaché, what cultural programs you plan bring to Soviet Union for people to enjoy?*" he said with a sly smile.

"As the United States Cultural Attaché, what type of cultural programs do you plan to bring to the Soviet Union for presentation?" the interpreter said diplomatically.

"Look, Boginin. We both know there will be no cultural programs. And, we both understand who we are. So let's cut the crap."

Connie sucked in her breath and shut her eyes. She couldn't believe what Richard just said. And, Tom thought I was going to start World War III.

"*You are biggest horse's ass ever come out of United States. It will pleasure to work with your stupidity.*"

Connie, let out a small laugh and quickly looked down at the floor. Keep your composure, kiddo. Don't let on you understand what he just said.

"You are the bi . . ." the interpreter stopped and began to cough. "I am so sorry. Something was in my throat."

Connie lowered her head again and bit her lip to now keep from laughing at what the interpreter was saying.

"You are the . . . er, a benefit. You are a benefit to your, ah, country." By this time, his face was deep red.

Richard just nodded and gave Mislav a superior smile. Mislav shook his head and stared to walk away. But, then he turned and added in English, "You know? You should give secretary raise."

He then bowed formally to Connie and said, "*Dovz vidanya*, Dear Lady."

Oh, what the hell. He knows now that I speak Russian. "*Dovsvidanya*, Mr. Boginin," Connie said in Russian.

Connie watched as he walked away. When he was out of earshot, Connie said, "Richard. You need to learn to speak Russian."

"Why should I bother to do that? We have inter-preters for that." he said.

Connie turned back to look at him. Oh, this is going to feel so good. And, he deserves this so much. She smiled broadly. "Because, Boginin just called you a horse's ass, Richard."

With that, she turned and went to join the raucous Italians.

CHAPTER 32

The CIA agent entered Joe Kaminsky's office as soon as he came into work. "Joe, Gregorovich wants to make contact with us. I saw his mark when I checked Gorky Park this morning. It wasn't there last night when the night agent made his rounds."

"Finally. I've been giving him time to cool down," Joe replied. "I'll pick him up when he leaves work tonight and follow him. Hopefully, he'll go straight to his mother's house and not waste time in the city. It will make things a lot easier. I wonder what he wants."

"Like all the others, he probably wants money," sneered the agent.

"Nah. Gregorovich doesn't strike me like that. And, watch the cynicism, kiddo. A dollar here buys a lot of information," Joe added.

Joe was sitting in his car outside of the Soviet Military building parking lot. He picked up Nicholas as he left the lot and started to head out of the city. Good. Just keep going and don't make any stops, Comrade.

As he was driving, he thought about how he was going to handle Nicholas tonight. I could be cool and detached, like he was wasting my time. But, we need him back. We can't get at Polakova without him. Angry? Truth be told, I am angry at him for not confiding in me about why he wanted to quit on us. On the other hand, I like the guy. Not just because he is dating my cousin. I liked him even before I knew about her. He's had a rough life – father died in the War when he was a kid. Mother lost her job. And, then he finds out his father was really murdered. And, the Soviets are so paranoid. They don't trust anyone, sometimes not even family members. Maybe, what he needs is a friend. Okay, I'll play this one by ear and let him set the tone and see what happens.

Joe tailed Nicholas to his mother's house and then continued on down the street. He made several turns to make sure he wasn't being followed. Returning to the house, he also checked for cars and people that seemed out of place to make sure Nicholas wasn't being watched either. Things looked normal. He parked his car around the corner, walked back to the house and knocked on the back door.

"Good evening, Comrade," he said as Nicholas answered the door.

When he entered, it was Nicholas who pulled the curtains on the kitchen windows. He turned and said, "The last time you were here, you checked to make sure there were no listening devices. Can you do that again, Comrade?"

"Of course," Joe said calmly as he began his check. What the heck is going on here, he thought.

"There doesn't appear to be any devices, Nicholas," he said upon returning to the kitchen. Nicholas was standing in the middle of the room. His hands were balled into fists. His jaw seemed to be clenched shut. The tension was obvious. Joe took that all in and knew what needed to be done. He sat down at the table and assumed a relaxed pose.

"Now tell me what's going on, my friend."

Nicholas began to pace. Several times he stopped, opened his mouth as if to speak then continued to pace again. Finally, he turned to Joe, paused and said, "Igor is setting me up just like he set up my father. I want to defect."

Joe nodded. He did not change his relaxed pose as he said, "Why do you think you are being set up, Nicholas?"

Nicholas pulled a folded document out of his breast pocket and handed it to Joe. "This is a document which allows me to enter the vaults that contain all of our top-secret, Soviet nuclear information. Igor gave it to me yesterday. He told me he wanted me to prepare a comprehensive paper on all of our nuclear capabilities to be presented to top, Soviet military personnel. The authorization has Igor's signature. But, the signature is a fake. Igor didn't sign this. Someone else did it for him."

For a brief moment, Joe used all his CIA training and every ounce of his self-control to continue to remain calm. His mind was racing. Nicholas was going to have access to all nuclear information. Holy shit. This is a gold mine. This information would put us so far ahead of the Soviets. How long do we have to do this? We definitely would have to get Gregorovich out. He swallowed and looked up at Nicholas.

"First of all, I think I need a shot of vodka," Joe gave a slight laugh. That did not seem to reduce the tension in Nicholas, but he did get up to get the bottle and two glasses.

"Now, tell me why you think this signature is a fake and why you think Igor is trying to set you up," Joe said as he poured the crystal liquid in the two glasses. He lifted his glass, raised it to Nicholas while looking him in the eye, the way any good Russian would. He downed the vodka in one swallow. It was the first time in his life he actually "needed" a shot of vodka.

Nicholas also downed his drink. "I have known Igor for years. I know what his signature looks like. This isn't it. I know the minute I walk out of the vault with copies of the nuclear documents, I will be arrested for treason. That is why I need to defect. As to why Igor wants me gone – it could be any number of reasons. Once I am gone, Igor will no longer have to be reminded about what he did to my father and mother. Seeing me everyday keeps the past alive for him. And, I know he is jealous of me. I am smarter than he is. Last month our Soviet Command Committee, what you call your Joint Chiefs of Staff, requested I accompany Igor to one of their meetings. I saw the hatred in his eyes when he told me they had asked me to attend."

Nicholas poured two more shots, raised his glass to Joe and said, "There is one more thing. I will not be defecting alone. There will be two other people that will be coming with me. I haven't told you about this. But, I will not go without my girlfriend. Her name is Anya Kaminsky. Actually, I am going to marry her, but not here. And, I know Anya will not leave without her grandmother."

Joe hadn't planned on drinking any more than the one shot of vodka tonight. But he found himself picking up the glass and downing this one as quickly as he had the first shot. Jeez, what other bombs is this guy going to drop on me, he thought.

"What do you mean, you can't get married here?"

Nicholas told Joe how Igor used Anya to follow him. He also assured him she saw nothing and reported nothing. That's why Igor called her off. She was useless to him. Now they could not risk being seen together.

"When does Igor want this report?"

"He said he wants it within two weeks. I have until the 6th to have it finished. He told me to go into the vaults tomorrow. Comrade, you have to help me. I refuse to allow Igor to essentially murder me the way he murdered my father. But, I don't know how to stop him."

Joe rubbed his hand over his face and sat forward with his elbows on his thighs. "Okay, Nicholas here's the deal. We will help you defect. But, you have to come out with something to offer us. That's the way it is. So, you do have to go into the vault and get as many nuclear documents as you can to bring with you."

Nicholas looked appalled. "You are sending me to my death."

Joe held up his hand. "Hear me out. We will have plans in place to get you out as quickly as possible once you have the documents. We won't let you sit here. The problem now is to buy you some time so we can get those plans in place. I don't want you to go into the vaults until we have a chance to do that."

"Tomorrow I want you to eat a big breakfast before you go to work. On your way in, I'll have one of my agents pass you a vial of medicine called Ipecac. It will make you very sick. Don't worry. It is not poison. In fact, we use Ipecac in the United States to flush out poisons from the body. An hour after you get to work, go in the bathroom and swallow the liquid, then go directly back to your desk. You have to be in the open where people will see you. About five minutes later, you will begin to throw up violently. This will give you the excuse to say you are sick and need to go home. Believe me, everyone will be glad to see you go. That will take care of Wednesday. You will call in sick on both Thursday and Friday. That will take you through the weekend and give us five days to get our plans in place."

"I know I must do it. But, I am going to make such a fool of myself." Nicholas just shook his head in misery.

"As for this Anya and her grandmother, Nicholas. I can't promise we will be able to get them out too." Although, every fiber of his being wanted to do just that. He wanted his grandmother and father to be able to see each other again.

"I will not go without them," Nicholas said firmly. "If you can't get them out with me, then there will be no nuclear documents. Do I make myself clear?"

"Where, ah, do they live? Tell me more about them, Nicholas," Joe said acting innocent. In truth, he probably knew more about them than Nicholas did.

CHAPTER 33

Joe's thoughts were coming at him like machine gun fire as he drove back to the U.S. Embassy that night. Along with replaying the things Nicholas had told him, he was thinking of all the things he had to get in place for Nicholas' defection. Three times he had to slow the car down. Since he was now under-cover with false documents, he had no diplomatic immunity if the police pulled him over for speed-ing. That's all he needed right now – to waste pre-cious time dealing with the Moscow police.

Upon returning to the Embassy, Joe went straight to the night duty officer. He had to locate Richard Morgan. This could not wait until morning. As Sta-tion Chief, Richard and Joe had to get on this right away. When he was told Richard was at a party at the Dutch Embassy, he sent a Marine sergeant to the Embassy with an urgent message requesting he return to the U.S. Embassy immediately.

Thirty minutes later, Richard stormed into Joe's office. "Who the hell do you think you are calling me out of an Embassy party. This had better be good," Richard sneered. "Get in my office and tell me what this is all about." He left Joe sitting with his mouth open in astonishment as he turned and walked back down the hall.

Well, Connie did say I probably wouldn't like him, Joe thought as he gathered all the notes he had been making and proceeded to Richard's office.

Once he was seated across from Richard, Joe told him everything about his meeting with Gregorovich including how he was going to have Nicholas take Ipecac to buy them some time for planning. Richard remained silent during Joe's entire explanation. He had his lips pursed together and was nodding his head when Joe ended.

"All right. Here's how it's going to be," Richard began. "We are going to get the nuclear documents, but there will be no defection."

"What?" Joe said completely caught off guard. "You can't do that."

"I can and I will. Getting the nuclear information will be a coup for me. But, if you think I am going to risk my career getting some two-bit informant out of the Soviet Union, think again, buddy boy. I am not jeopardizing everything I've worked for, for some Russian hustler."

"Richard, for God sake, if we abandon Gregorovich now, no Soviet informant will ever trust us again. Are you nuts? If this gets out, we stand to lose fifty of our current informants, not to mention getting any new ones in the future. If you don't help Gregorovich defect it will take us years to repair this mess. You can't do this," Joe said as he slammed his hand on Richard's desk.

"I know why you're doing this, Kaminsky. I've read the file. You just want to get your little granny and cousin out. Gregorovich has nothing to do with this," Richard sneered.

Joe took in a breath of air and let it out. He could not believe this. This conversation seemed surreal. No Station Chief would ever act like this. Richard had to be the dumbest person he had ever dealt with. Joe had never been as angry with anyone in his entire life. He had to get out of this office. He would come back in the morning to talk to Richard;

after he had a chance to calm down, because right now he wanted to beat the crap out of him.

Joe gathered up his notes and left Richard's office. When he got back to his office, he knew he wouldn't be able to concentrate until he got the anger out. He began doing stretching exercises. After five minutes he started to run in place. These were things the CIA taught recruits to relieve stress in the field. He kept running in place for the next ten minutes. He ended with deep breathing for two minutes. Finally, he felt better and knew he could continue planning.

He sat down and added to his notes until four in the morning. He needed to sleep. He would use one of the Embassy bedrooms. After he locked his office door, he stopped in the office of the CIA's night agent. He gave him instructions to deliver the Ipecac to Nicholas that morning. Then he climbed the stairs to the spare bedroom.

There is nothing more I can do for now, Joe thought as he laid on the bed and stared at the ceiling. I need sleep more than I need to worry. He set the alarm for 8 a.m., turned over and went to sleep.

Connie was in Richard's office staring at him with her mouth slightly open. He started the conversation by telling Connie his wife would not be coming to Moscow during his assignment. Then, he told her he wanted to resume their relationship again. He asked her to have dinner with him that night.

"Do you honestly think I would be that dumb to have anything to do with you ever again, Richard? You married another woman two days after we had gone to bed together for heavens sake. How loathsome is that? Trusting you was biggest mistake of my life."

"Well, it couldn't have been that bad because you sure knew how to respond to me in bed, Connie," Richard said with a smirk. "So why not go back to what we had in Washington?"

"Not ever, Richard. Not here. Not anywhere," Connie spat.

Richard's eyes hardened as he looked at Connie. "Then, I think you should request another posting. You obviously don't know how to fit in. And, besides, secretaries are a dime a dozen."

"Just to let you know, I've already put in for a transfer." Richard seemed stunned to hear that.

"I did it last week. I should hear something by the middle of next month."

"If there's nothing else, I need to get back to my desk," she said as icily as she could. Yeah, right. Like the tone of my voice is going to do any good, she thought as she walked to the door. If only I could hurt him like he hurt me. But, Richard is so egotistical and obtuse. Nothing can touch him.

When she stepped out, Joe was standing at her desk. He looked very agitated. "Morning, Joe. How are you?"

"Is he in?" Joe said tersely.

"Sure, I'll let him know you're here," Connie said as she picked up her phone.

"Don't bother." Joe opened Richard's door and went in. Connie was left with the receiver to her ear and her finger on the dial. What is going on, she frowned.

Ten minutes later, Joe slammed the door as he came storming out of Richard's office. His face was red. Connie was stunned. She had never seen anyone so angry.

"Joe, what happened? What's the matter?"

"That son-of-a-bitch is going to ruin our entire operation here. That's what the matter is," he said as he stalked out of Connie's office slamming her door too.

She grabbed two cups of coffee and went to find Joe. He was in his office seated at his desk when she found him. He seemed completely oblivious that she had entered.

"I come in peace, friend. And, I come bearing gifts," she added as she set one of the cups on Joe's desk. "I hope you like cream and sugar."

He looked startled; then he gave her a slight smile. "Sit down. And, thanks," he said as he took a sip of the coffee.

"Joe, what's going on? What happened back there?"

It took a few moments for Joe to compose himself. Finally he began to tell Connie all that had happened since last evening.

By the time he was finished, Joe's teeth were clenched. "And, that son-of-a-bitch can't see the harm he's doing. The idiot is just worried about his damn career! How the hell did he ever get appointed to be Station Chief? That's what I want to know."

Connie did not reply immediately, but sat thinking quietly. After a while, she raised an eyebrow and asked, "Joe, do you have any vacation time left?"

"Vacation time? What the hell does that have to do with this?" Joe replied irritably.

"Well, do you?"

"Yeah, I still have a couple of days left. So what?" He looked at her like she was nuts.

Connie smiled as she reached for a pen and paper on his desk. She wrote down a name and address and handed the paper to Joe.

"Can you be at this address at 2:00 o'clock tomorrow afternoon?"

"What the hell is this? This is a café in Paris for crying out loud."

"I know. There is someone in Paris who may be able to help us, Joe. I think you should meet him."

CHAPTER 34

Once the plane out of Moscow to Brussels left Soviet air space, Connie breathed a sigh of relief. Even though she had diplomatic immunity, she had heard too many stories from other Embassy people who had been hassled by the border guards as they were leaving the Soviet Union. This was one time when neither she nor Joe could afford one second of delay. She hoped Joe was having the same good luck on his flight to Amsterdam. He had the longer flight and the longest drive to Paris.

It took me a while to convince Joe to meet with David Levi in Paris. I can certainly understand why he was reluctant about agreeing to waste precious time flying off to France, she thought. They only had five days before Nicholas had to return to work and more than likely go into the nuclear vaults. But, without the okay from Richard, Joe's hands were literally tied from helping Nicholas and his cousin and grandmother escape.

Joe finally agreed, because he was worried about asking for help from the other Embassies in Moscow. The more people who knew what he was trying to do, the more possibility of leaks pointing to Nicholas. The KGB would kill Nicholas for sure. And, he was also worried that word might get back to Richard about Joe's plans to get him out.

"Please God, let David still be in Paris," she whispered. This whole plan hinges on him now. Since Israel isn't recognized by the Soviets, they don't have an Embassy in Moscow – no leaks, no word getting back to Richard. But, they had no way to try to get in touch with David either. Therefore, she and Joe had to leave the country to contact him. We want to explain all the details to David, so he can go to the Mossad. I hope they agree to help us.

As she looked out the window, she went over the plans they had made during the past, six hours. Well, actually, the plans Joe had made. My contribution was my past association with David and the Mossad.

I will check into a hotel in Brussels and call Aaron Zuker in Tel Aviv to ask him to locate David and tell him to meet us at the café in Paris. Tom told me about Aaron. But, I didn't have his phone number. It was Joe who got it from his contact at the British Embassy.

Dumb me. I was going to call Aaron from my apartment and tell him what I wanted. Then I was just going to fly off to Paris for the meet. Joe turned white when I told him what I planned to do. Connie chuckled at that.

"First of all," Joe hissed. "All international phone calls from the Soviet Union are monitored. You never ever make any clandestine calls from here, even from our Embassy. And, second, you never ever fly directly to your destination. All the border guards in the entire Soviet Union are under the command of the KGB. You said you foiled the Russian attempt by the KGB when you were in Paris the last time. Well, kiddo, you are now on their radar. Fly directly to Paris and you might as well put a sign on your forehead. It will be so obvious."

Thank goodness for Joe. I'd probably be in jail right now if it wasn't for him. It was his plan we should each fly to a nearby city and then rent a car and drive to Paris. After our meeting with David, we will drive back to Brussels and Amsterdam and fly back out. If all goes well, we will be back in the Soviet Union early Friday morning.

And, Richard, the dumb cluck, presented no problem for either of us. I told him I needed a few days off to calm down. Probably adding the retort – "Who knows, Richard, you may get lucky with a temporary secretary", made him buy my story. Joe told him he was going to meet his father who was coming to Amsterdam on a short vacation. The jerk bought into that too. Here is the CIA coup of a lifetime, where time is absolutely crucial, and Richard didn't even think in those terms. He just let Joe leave. Oh, Tom. How I miss you.

CHAPTER 35

Connie's plane landed in late afternoon. By the time she got her luggage and went through customs, it was nearly 5:00 p.m. She took a cab to the hotel, which took 30 minutes. At the front desk, she arranged for a rental car to be available tomorrow morning at 7:00 a.m. It would be a four-hour drive to Paris allowing for the border stop between Belgium and France. Connie didn't envy poor Joe. He had at least a nine-hour drive from Amsterdam. I hope he got a chance to sleep on the plane, she thought.

When she got to her room, she decided to call Aaron Zucker in Tel Aviv even though it was already close to 7:00 p.m. there. The original plan was that she would call Tel Aviv early tomorrow morning before she set off for Paris. But, she was too nervous to wait until the morning. If I can't arrange to meet David in Paris, this whole thing will fall apart, she thought.

Hopefully, if Aaron isn't in his office, my call will be transferred to a switchboard. That way, they might be able to page him or I can leave my name and hotel phone number.

Connie sat on the bed, picked up the receiver and crossed her fingers. While she was dialing, she whispered, "Well, here goes nothing."

On the fourth ring, a gentleman answered the phone in far off Tel Aviv.

"Shalom."

Connie realized she had been holding her breath and giving the receiver a white knuckler.

"I would like to speak to Mr. Aaron Zucker please."

"Who is this?" the man answered none too kindly in English now.

"This is Connie O'Rourke. I was Tom Bursak's secretary. I am trying to locate Mr. Zucker." She thought she heard the man suck in a breath of air.

He paused for a moment then said, "This is Aaron Zucker."

"Oh, thank goodness, Mr. Zucker. I was afraid that you wouldn't be in your office at this time of night. I'm so glad to have reached you. Is David Levi still in Paris? It's very important I get in contact with him. And, I really don't have much time. I am so sorry to put you though all this trouble. But, if you could just help me, I . . . "

"Slow down, slow down, dear lady. First of all, I have no idea who this David Levi is. And, second, how did you get this phone number?" Aaron asked.

Oh lord, I blew it, Connie thought frantically. I know Tom said his Mossad contact was Aaron Zucker. And, Joe's counterpart at the British Embassy gave us this phone number. This has got to be the right man.

"It's very important I get a message to David Levi in Paris – at least I hope he is still in Paris. This will be awful if he isn't. Please tell me you are the Aaron Zucker who knew my boss, Tom Bursak and that you can help me," Connie pleaded.

"Yes, I am Aaron Zucker. But, I am sorry, dear lady, I must tell you again. I don't know this David Levi, so I cannot help you," Aaron replied. Then he added, "By the way, you did not answer my question. How did you get this phone number?"

Connie tried to calm herself. She took in a breath of air and let it out. "I'm sorry. You're right. I'm so nervous. I've never done anything like this before." Connie continued in a more rational manner, "Okay. First of all, I know your name, because I worked for Tom Bursak. Mr. Zucker, you do know Tom died of a heart attack last month don't you?"

Connie paused and waited for a reply. But, Aaron remained silent. So she continued.

"Then when we realized we had to reach David, we got your phone number from our British counterpart in Moscow."

"We?" Aaron jumped on that word.

"We? Oh, Joe my co-worker in Moscow and I," Connie replied. Again, Connie paused and again Aaron remained silent. Oh, this man is really starting to bug me Connie fumed. Nuts to this!

"Look, Mr. Zucker, even though I work in the same business as you do, I'm really not good at being cryptic. I know who you are and I know you know who I am, because according to Tom, you are the one who sent David Levi to Washington to meet me."

"Where are you calling from?" Aaron asked.

"I'm calling from my hotel room in Brussels," Connie answered.

"I thought you said this David Levi was in Paris. Why are you in Brussels?"

""He is the one in Paris! I'm in Brussels trying to get to Paris." Connie realized the pitch of her voice was rising. "At least, I hope David is still in Paris," she said less snappishly.

"I am sorry, Madame, but I simply cannot help you. As I said in the beginning, I simple don't know the gentleman," Aaron insisted.

"Ugh. Mr. Zucker, you are making this very, very difficult. Let's try this again another way. Hypothetically . . . if you knew David Levi, would you get a message to him for me?" Connie said running out of patience.

"Oh, well, putting it that way. Hypothetically, if I did know this David Levi, then yes, I would pass along your message to him," Aaron responded. "By the way, just what would the message be?"

"Hypothetically, my message for David would be – Sugar is calling in her marker. Please meet me tomorrow at 2:00 p.m. exactly at the café we met at last September," Connie told him. "Do you want me to repeat that?"

"No, no. I have it," he replied.

"Can I also give you my phone number here in Brussels? But, I should tell you I will be leaving by 7:00 a.m. tomorrow morning to drive to Paris," Connie added.

"Sure. Why not? I will write that down too," answered Aaron.

After Connie had given him the number, he said, "Well, hypothetically, I hope this all works out for you. But, what do I know? I'm just an old man with seven grandchildren."

Connie gave a startled cry. Tears began to well up. "Oh, Mr. Zucker, Tom said you always say that."

Both were quiet for a moment. Then, Aaron said quietly, "Miss O'Rourke, hypothetically, if I had known Tom Bursak, I would miss him very much."

"Shalom, Mr. Zucker. Maybe someday you can show me a picture of your grandchildren," Connie said.

"Shalom, Miss O'Rourke. If we ever meet, I will be sure to do that." With that, Aaron hung up the phone.

CHAPTER 36

"Yeah, same to you, buddy," said Joe as he cut off a French driver who proceeded to give him a non-welcoming gesture out of his driver's window. Joe grinned to himself. He was having the time of his life driving through the narrow and crowded streets of Paris. This was just like being home driving through Brooklyn, he thought. The hustle and bustle was a welcome change from the bleak streets of Moscow. Plus, even though it was the beginning of winter here too, there wasn't the gloom that permeated that Soviet city. The lights in the apartment windows and shops sparkled in the crisp air. The people dressed in colorful clothing. As they walked in this city, they talked and smiled and greeted one another – a big no-no in Moscow.

It was now shortly after 12:30 p.m. in Paris and Joe was on his way to meet Connie and her Mossad friend for their rendezvous. Joe smiled again at this. If this were Moscow, I would say, "meet", but here in Paris I must say "rendezvous". His original plan when he arrived in Amsterdam yesterday was to get a hotel room to get some sleep then leave this morning around 4:00 a.m. for Paris. But, he had a chance to sleep a couple of hours on the plane. So, when he arrived in Amsterdam, he decided to get a car and drive through the night then grab the few hours of sleep in a youth hostel here. As it turned out, that was a good idea, because for the most part he was alone on the roads last night and was able to drive much faster than during the day. He made it to Paris in 7 ½ hours instead of nine.

As an added bonus, this morning he had time to drive around and see some of the sights of Paris. The enormity of the base of Eiffel Tower was awesome. To think that was the tallest structure in the world a mere 67 years ago at the turn of the century, and back then the Parisians hated it. They wanted it torn down. Notre Dame Cathedral was a disappointment though. He had time to go inside of it. It was very plain. He had seen more spectacular churches in other European countries. He was going to write it off as another tourist trap until he overheard one of the passing guides mention that Notre Dame was the first church built with vaulted ceilings. All others then copied the style. He looked at it anew and marveled at the French ingenuity.

He anticipated getting to the appointed café in about 20 minutes. That would give him time to reconnoiter. He wanted to check out the café and the area. Who was going in and out? What would be good escape routes? Would they have privacy to talk?

David Levi also came early to the café to check it out. As he was walking around the neighborhood, he spotted a non-descript man across the street. He seemed out of place. Don't tell me the KGB learned about this meeting too, he worried. David studied the man as he began to tail him. The guy was wearing rumpled European clothing, but his shoes weren't European. They looked different than what men wore here. It was his walk that alerted David to keep a watch on him. The man crossed the street to David's side, so he then stopped and looked in a shop window. He waited to see what the man would do. The man continued down the street and turned the corner toward the café. David increased his pace. When he came around the corner, he slowed back down. He saw the man had remained on the same side of the street as the café. Then he slowed down and seemed to study it as he went by. Stranger and stranger, David thought as he crossed the street and stood by a tree to light a cigarette all the while keeping the other man in view.

The man speeded up after he passed the café. Three buildings down, he quickly turned into a narrow alleyway. David threw his cigarette down and ran across the street while dodging on-coming cars. When he got to the alley, the man was nowhere to be seen. It was a long, narrow passageway between a series of old buildings. Shit, I lost him, David thought as he cautiously began walking down the passage while hugging the wall on the right side. As he passed a recessed doorway, David heard the man before he could turn and react. The man grabbed David's right arm and yanked it behind him. He then had his left arm around David's throat as he came up behind him.

"All right, bozo. You want to tell me why you're following me," the man hissed in David's ear as he tightened his grip on David's arm.

"I have no idea what you mean, Monsieur," David answered in French.

"Cut the crap, asshole. You're about as French as I am. Now one more time, why are you following me?"

David kicked the side of the man's leg, and then came down hard on the top of his foot. The man loosened his grip allowing David to turn and grab the man by the shoulders. In a flash he pulled him toward himself and then turned and the man's momentum kept him also in the turn. He had the man down on the ground. Holding the man's arm behind his back and pressing his knee into the man's spine, it was David's turn to ask the questions.

"Just why do you think I am following you, Gonif?" hissed David.

"Gonif? Oh, hell. Get off of me, you Jewish idiot. We're here for the same reason," the man replied. "I'm a friend of your two o'clock appointment, Dumbo."

David was so startled at the reference to two o'clock that he started to release the man. As soon as he did, the man turned on his side, reach up and grab David by the shoulder. With a pull and a twist, he flipped David flat on the ground. The man sat up and was breathing deeply with a smile on his face while staring down at David lying on his back.

"I'm Joe and you are the all mighty David, I presume?" said Joe shaking his head. "Pretty dumb for Mossad to get caught like that."

"Yeah, well, pretty dumb to stand so close so that I was able to get CIA on the ground," David said as he rubbed his right arm and smiled.

Joe stood and offered a helping hand to David. "See anything of interest I should know about?"

"Other than you? No," David said as he stood up.

David spotted Connie as she arrived at the café at 2:00 p.m. on the dot. He watched her as she looked around the café. Nothing's changed, he thought. I still want her. When she spotted David, a look of intense relief crossed her face. She smiled broadly at him as she walked to the table. His heart seemed to skip a beat. David stood and pulled out a chair for her. When she reached the table, he kissed her on the cheek.

"Hello, David. I am so glad you got my message." Then she looked at Joe perplexed. "Joe. You got here. But, how did you know this was David? And, why do the two of you look so grungy? It looks like you two have been in a fight or something."

"Ah, well, we, ah, didn't want to stand out. We just wanted to look like one of the guys. Right, David?" Joe replied. David shook his head in agreement, as if he didn't want to tell her how ineptly they had met either.

"Look, Connie, we decided that we are just going to have a cup of coffee here and then go to my apartment to talk. This isn't a good place for it," David said.

"Oh, right. I can see what you mean," she answered as she looked around the small café. Since it was winter, all the tables that had been outside when she was here the last time were now pulled inside making it extremely crowded.

"Connie, I still can't believe you just pick up the phone and called Aaron Zucker directly," said David as he shook his head and smiled at her. "That number is a closely guarded secret. Few people, even in Israel, know it."

"Well, how secret can it be? My boss had it and the British guy in Moscow was able to get it. And besides, what else was I supposed to do? I didn't know where you were or how to contact you. So, I just called your boss – and here we are," Connie smiled as she looked around David's apartment.

"Yeah, listen, enough of the chit-chat. We need to tell you why we're here. We need your help and we don't have a lot of time. In fact, we only have hours. Nothing more," Joe chimed in. They were sitting at David's kitchen table.

David had to drag his eyes away from Connie and concentrate on Joe. "Okay. What's the urgency of getting in contact with me?" David said as he leaned back in his chair and waited for Joe to continue.

David watched Joe intently as he slowly began reconstructing the events of the passed few days. David realized Joe was only telling him as much as he could. He didn't use the names of the spy or the Soviet military man, but referred to them as the Russian guy and a high-ranking Russian military man. He also included a woman and her grand-mother, again no names, as additional assets that had to come out. When Joe finished, David sat quietly for a few moments.

Then he said, "So you're telling me even though the Russian guy is going to risk his life getting nuclear secrets, this *putz* of a boss intends to leave him hanging out there with no U.S. help what-so-ever?" He simply couldn't believe it.

"That's about it," Joe responded softly. "I can't let that happen, David. That's not who I am. I can't let the CIA sink so low on this one. I'd rather lose my job than let this guy be caught by the KGB. We both know the torture he would have to endure before they would finally kill him. We need the Mossad's help to get these three people out."

"Will you help us, David," Connie asked as she leaned across the table staring at David.

He said nothing. His mind was churning. His gaze was fixed on the wall directly behind Joe.

"All right. Let me see what I can do. I need to make a phone call to a, ah secret phone number in Tel Aviv that few people know about." He looked at Connie and gave her a wink. "It should take about a half an hour; and, you two need to leave my apartment while I'm making the call. I want to be able to speak freely."

"I understand," Joe said as he rose and nodded to Connie.

Connie smiled at David and quietly said, "Thank you."

David hung up the phone only moments before Connie and Joe returned and were knocking on his door. They are going to explode when I tell them how the Mossad intends to help them, he thought as went to let them in. Once they were seated, he looked at both of them. Then he began.

"The Mossad has agreed to help you get these Russians out of the Soviet Union. But, we want something. Joe, you of all people should understand. In the espionage game, nothing is free. First, you have to give us the names of all the players in this situation. We will need as much background as we can get in order to help you pull this off. And, second." David paused and looked across the table at Joe. Here it comes, David thought. Here is where Joe is going to lose it.

"And, second, we will be the ones who will take the Russian guy out, not you, because we want the original nuclear documents when he comes out. We will give you copies of everything he brings – but we want the originals."

Joe flew out of his chair knocking it over as he did. "What! Are you nuts? No way are we going to agree to that. We've been handling this guy for months. We're not giving up what we worked so hard for. And, further more, we have no guarantee you guys will give us everything he brings out. No. No way. No how. This discussion is over. Come on, Connie, we're leaving."

Connie didn't rise. She remained seated. "No, Joe. Give him what he wants." A mean smile appeared on her pursed lips.

She raised her chin and looked at Joe out of the corner of her eyes.

"Don't you see, Joe? If you do that, not only will Nicholas, Anya and your grandmother get out, but it will bring down Richard Morgan at the same time." Her smile turned to a smirk. The two men were stunned by the look on her face.

"Holy cow, Connie. What exactly did Richard do to you?" Joe asked flabbergasted. Connie did not respond to his question.

"You can say Richard wouldn't allow you to help Nicholas escape, which is true. He tied your hands, another truth. Nicholas got scared. He had no choice, so he . . . was the one who turned to the

Jews to get him out. Then, it was the Russian Jews who contacted the Mossad. And, out of the goodness of fair play, the Mossad gave the CIA photocopies of the documents."

"And, David," Connie said forcefully. "I want your word that the Mossad will give *all the copies* of what Nicholas' brings. Look at it this way, if you don't, Israel certainly is in no position to go to war with the Soviet Union. But, we are. Therefore, we need all the nuclear information. No holding back."

Joe looked at her admiringly. Not a bad negotiator. For a moment he became lost in thought and then he said slowly, "I have to admit Morgan doesn't belong in the CIA. He's putting everything in jeopardy by this." He bent down and set his chair upright, "All right. Let's at least talk."

For the next three hours, David worked with Joe and Connie. He and Joe put forth ideas and then dissected them, discarding those that were either unworkable or would take too long to put into place. When all of them felt they had a plan that was doable, they sat quietly. Nothing had been written down.

"Are we all clear on what each of us has to do?" David asked them. Joe and Connie nodded slowly.

"I wish we had more time. This whole thing seems to come down to almost minutes."

"You're the one who is going to get Gregorovich out of Russia, David? How the heck are you going to get into the Soviet Union to begin with?" Connie asked.

"Let me worry about that, Connie," he answered.

"I need to use your phone, David," Joe said. "I have to call my Dad to make sure he's at the airport to meet his mother and niece when they come out. I can't make this call in Moscow, because of all the listening devices the Soviets have. But, later I can make a cryptic call from Moscow letting him know exactly which city they will be flying to." He started to laugh. "Wait till I tell my dad this. He thinks I have some boring job with the State Department."

After Joe's phone call to his dad, he and Connie prepared to leave. He shook David's hand and thanked him as he stepped out into the hall. Connie hugged David fiercely as she was leaving.

"Thank you David," she said.

David held on to her arm and stopped her at the door. "Connie, can I have a word with you?"

"Of course." She remained standing in the doorway as Joe continued walking down the hall.

David held onto her arm and looked at her. "When this is all over, I am going to come and get you, because I intend to marry you."

"What?" Connie stood there gaping at him. David kissed her soundly, gave her a wink and closed the door softly.

Good grief, I never expected this to happen, Connie thought as she walked slowly down the hall. Who would have thought, my very first marriage proposal given at the end of a clandestine meeting to get people and nuclear secrets out of the Soviet Union. Connie, my girl, you do lead a very interesting life. She smiled as she walked to catch up with Joe. Besides, I'm sure David was only joking when he said he wanted to marry me.

CHAPTER 37

"Chinese Fire Drill. I don't have time for this idiocy," Joe muttered as he pulled his car into a parking space next to the apartment building. As a teenager, doing a Chinese Fire Drill was fun. Stop the car in the middle of the street. Everyone jump out and run around the car to change places. Then everyone jump back in and take off again. He could remember laughing hysterically with his friends as they performed that dumb trick. But, today time was at a premium. He needed to meet with Gregorovich as soon as possible.

Here in Moscow, Joe knew he was under constant surveillance by the KGB. Every time he stepped out of the Embassy, even if it was only for lunch, he was followed. In order to get rid of the tail when he needed to, he always had to spend at least an hour losing them. Hence, the Chinese Fire Drill as one of his predecessor's dubbed the procedure.

Usually, they did this with one or two agents. The CIA had numerous entrance and exit points throughout Moscow they used to lose a tail. The procedure was simple: the agent wanting to lose a tail would drive to an appointed place – a café, an apartment or office building, a large market place. The second agent would be waiting at the place wearing the identical clothes of the first agent. Once the first agent entered, the second agent would wait for a short interval. Then he would walk out, get into the first agent's car, and drive away. In the mean time, the first agent would change clothes. The change of clothes would be simple – turn a reversible coat inside out, change hats or add a different colored wig or glasses. The first agent would then leave by an opposite door, get into the car left by the second agent, and drive to the meet.

Today, they were doing four exchanges so Joe could reach Gregorovich. He was on his last exchange. He felt he was no longer being followed. But, they couldn't take any chances. So, muttering under his breath, he got out of the car and walked to the final exchange.

It had taken nearly three hours for Joe to reach Nicholas' house. He knew he would not be sleeping tonight. There was still too much left to do. Hopefully, his agents would be working on contacting their counterparts at the other Embassies. Interesting to note, even though he told them they would be working without the knowledge of Richard Morgan, not one of his agents refused to help put the plans in place. They were willing to risk their jobs, because they all understood what was at stake if they didn't get Gregorovich out, even if that bastard, Morgan, didn't.

Nicholas opened the door before Joe even had a chance to knock. "Come in Comrade. I was starting to worry when I did not hear from you for the last two days,"

"We are still putting plans in place, Nicholas. I will tell you what must be done by you within the next three days." After the security check of the house, Joe took a seat at the kitchen table and motioned for Nicholas to do the same.

Joe began speaking quietly, "We are going to get your girlfriend and her grandmother out also."

Nicholas breathed a sigh of relief. "Thank goodness. How do we leave? When do we leave?"

"Hold on, Nicholas. It won't be that simple. First of all, Anya and her grandmother will be flying out of Moscow to the West." Joe had no intention of telling him they would be flying to Helsinki or that Joe's father would be waiting at the Helsinki airport to meet his own mother and niece when they arrived. When he had called his dad in Paris and was free to talk, he told him about the plan to get them out. His dad could not stop crying. It had been thirty years since he had seen his mother. At the beginning they corresponded, but in 1959, the Soviets cracked down on letters mailed out or received from outside of the Soviet Union. All correspondence between his dad and his mother stopped after that. He thought his mother had died.

Tomorrow he would be calling him from Moscow with a cryptic message to let him know the city would be Helsinki and the exact time his dad should meet them. On the Paris phone call, Joe had stressed the importance to his dad of not making any mention of Joe's job or any mention of either his mother or niece when he called. He just hoped his Dad remembered that when he called him tomorrow.

"You will be leaving the Soviet Union by car. You will drive south and have to walk from Bulgaria into the northern part of Greece. It will take at least two days of driving and then most of the night to walk across. You have to leave by a southern route, because the western routes are covered with snow. The border guards will see your footprints before you even get near the border. You would never make it. That's why we chose Bulgaria.

"Stop. Why can't I fly out with them? You say you will get Anya and her grandmother out. But, how can I be sure you will keep your word? I want assurance they will be safe," Nicholas said.

Joe stared at him. How much do I tell him? Nothing. If he is caught before this is over, the KGB will surely torture him until they learn all there is to know. Anya and his grandmother will be leaving a few days after Nicholas is taken out. They can't be put in harm's way now.

"They will be gotten out, Nicholas. I give you my word on that. You are too well known. There is no way we can get you out of the Soviet Union on an airplane. Trying to leave with Anya and her grandmother would put them in jeopardy. Let me explain how everything is going to work then you can ask your questions. Okay?"

"All right, I am sorry. Please continue," Nicholas reluctantly agreed.

Joe began to tell him the plan. He spoke for over an hour. Then he spent the next hour answering all of Nicholas' questions. He made one amendment to the plans, however. He needed to keep Nicholas focused.

"I understand how important it is for you to know Anya is being helped. So, here's what we'll do. She will call you after she has made contact with our, ah, agent." Joe smiled internally. The "agent" was going to be Connie; one, because she spoke Russian; and two, because she was a woman. Everyone felt Anya and her grandmother would feel safer with Connie.

"If Anya agrees with our plans to fly her and her grandmother to the West, she will ask you if you remembered to buy flowers for Ivana's Name Day. That will be your assurance she understands and agrees. And, you need to assure Anya that you too agree with the plan to get you out of the Soviet Union. So, you will simply answer you bought the flowers and will be bringing them tomorrow. Say goodbye to each other and hang up. Do not under any circumstances say anything else. We have no idea if anyone will be listening in on this phone call.

You say Igor will probably set you up for treason. We don't know if he has contacted the KGB yet or not. We are hoping he won't do anything for a few days after you come out of the vault."

Joe watched Nicholas close his eyes and turn pale. Poor guy, Joe thought. "Nicholas, I want you to get as many pictures of the nuclear documents as you can when you go into the vault on Monday."

Joe removed a pen from his breast pocket. It was a camera that also worked as a pen. He showed Nicholas how to take pictures with it. "Take as many pictures of the nuclear documents as you can. We want to know where they are stored; where and how they are made; and, whether there are plans to arm satellites. Try to go into the vault Monday afternoon, because we will be getting you out that night. We don't want to wait any longer than that once you have the pictures."

When Joe was finished, Nicholas looked down at the floor for a moment then looked up at Joe. "And, you think what you will be doing after I leave will point to Igor? Are you sure all this will bring him down, because that is the only thing I have wanted ever since I contacted you."

Joe leaned over and put his hand on Nicholas' shoulder. "Destroying Igor has been the whole point of everything we are doing. Don't worry, my friend, your father did not die in vain."

As Joe was speaking to Nicholas, an attaché from the Danish government arrived at the Moscow airport from Copenhagen. He had a briefcase handcuffed to his wrist. He went through customs receiving dirty looks from the guards. But, they let him pass without incident. The man took a taxi to the Danish Embassy. In the back seat of the taxi he quietly removed the handcuffs from the briefcase and his wrist. When he arrived, he got out and paid the driver. As the taxi took off down the street he walked up to one of the Soviet guards stationed outside of the Embassy gate.

"Excuse me," the man said in simplistic Russian. "Can you please to speak to me where is hotel? I ask taxi people, but my Russian not good."

The guard told him a hotel was two blocks down and to the right three more blocks.

"Thank you. Thank you," the man said bowing as he started down the street. He walked the two blocks then turned right. After walking one more block, David Levi got into a car parked at the curb. He turned over his briefcase, handcuffs, and the passport he had been carrying to the driver of the car. The driver then handed him a new suitcase and a new Russian passport as he pulled away from the curb. He was driven to the Jewish sector or pogrom on the south side of Moscow.

CHAPTER 38

Connie knocked on the apartment door. Anya opened it and looked at Connie questioningly. Connie smiled and whispered, "I am a friend of Nicholas Gregorovich. May I come in to talk, Anya?" Now Anya looked frightened as she held the door open.

"You know who I am?" she whispered back. "You are not Russian, yet you speak Russian. Why? Who are you? What do you want?" Anya asked as Connie entered and she closed the door. By now her grandmother came into the hallway.

"What's wrong? Are you hurting my granddaughter?" said the older woman raising her fist at Connie.

Jeez, I'm going to be flattened by a crazy, old, Russian lady, Connie thought. She held up her hands. "Whoa. Take it easy. I'm not going to hurt anyone. Anya, can we sit down while I speak to you – privately? Please, this is important."

Anya hesitated. She finally nodded her head. "Grandmother, go into the kitchen while I speak to this lady."

"No. I am not leaving you alone with this prostitute," the grandmother said as she pointed a finger at Connie. Connie squinted back at the grandmother. Prostitute! Joe's grandmother or not, I'm going to give this *babushka* one swift kick in the rear for that remark.

Anya nodded and motioned that Connie should come into the living room. "Grandmother, please. Go sit in the kitchen. I'll be all right. Make us some tea."

When they were seated, Connie smiled at Anya. When in doubt, make it short and sweet, she thought. "Anya, my name is Connie O'Rourke. I work at the American Embassy. We are helping Nicholas leave the Soviet Union. But, he says he will not go without you and your grandmother. I am here to help the two of you leave."

Anya gasped as tears started to form in her eyes. "How do you know this? He is in danger, isn't he?

What has Igor done to him?" she asked Connie as she wiped the tears.

"Anya, we are doing everything we can to make sure he is safe. And, we want to make sure you are safe too. That's why I'm here."

"Why are you doing this for Nicholas and for us. I need to know why," Anya said.

Apparently Nicholas had not told her about bringing out nuclear secrets. Just as well. The less she knows, the safer she will be. But, she agreed with Anya. She needed to know why. But how much do I tell her?

"Anya, I understand you read the letter written by Igor to Joseph Stalin. And, I also know how Igor threatened you. He is an evil man who needs to be stopped. Nicholas is helping us do that. Will you let me tell you the plans we have to get you out of the country? When I am through you have to make a decision whether to go or to stay. I must tell you, if you choose to stay, Nicholas will stay also. He will not leave without you. Please just listen to what I have to say."

Anya lowered her head and said softly, "All right. Please tell me everything."

"Good. And, Grandmother, come in here. I know you are listening to everything we are saying," Connie looked back at the doorway and smiled as Anya's grandmother peaked around the corner. When she was seated next to Anya, Connie began.

"We are going to get you out of the Soviet Union by plane. The two of you will fly from Moscow to Helsinki. You both will be traveling with Finnish passports. Next Tuesday, you will go to the airport at 1:30 p.m. You will enter the terminal, but not to get on a plane. There will be passengers coming off a plane from Helsinki. Join their group as they leave the terminal. You will be picked up by an Embassy car in front of the terminal and taken to the Finnish Embassy here in Moscow. If anyone is watching, they will think you just arrived from Finland and are visiting. Once inside the Embassy, you will stay there for the next two days. On Friday, you will be driven back to the airport when you will board the real plane for Helsinki. This time, I will be at the airport when you arrive. I will get into the same boarding line behind you and fly out with you."

"We know you can speak some Finnish, because of your mother, Anya. However, we want you to speak only Russian if someone questions you as you go through the departure gate. Don't speak perfect Russian. Make a few mistakes. If asked why you are speaking Russian and not Finnish, just tell them you are with the Finnish government and as a courtesy you prefer to speak the language of the country. Grandma, we want you to pretend you are hard of hearing if anyone questions you. Make sure you always look confused if anyone talks to you. Anya, you will say that your grandmother is hard of hearing and you will answer for her."

"Now we need to make you two look as non-Russian as we can. Therefore, the people at the Finnish Embassy will dress you in Western clothing – that includes nylons, makeup and new hairdos. You will also be traveling on new Finish passports."

"Will Nicholas be coming with us?" Anya asked.

"No. Nicholas will be leaving by a different route. He will be leaving a few days before you. Now, one more thing, Anya; you can't just disappear. You need an excuse for not being seen for a few days. Therefore, on Monday morning at work, we want you to ask for a few days off. Tell them your grandmother got very sick over the weekend; and, you need to be home to take care of her. But, we want you to also call your friend, Katrina. Tell her your grandmother really isn't sick. But, you couldn't tell the people at work the real reason. The real reason, you are going away for a few days, is because you broke up with Nicholas and don't want to see him anymore. Say he has been acting crazy. Something is wrong; and, you don't like the way he has been acting. If she questions you, just say you don't know what is wrong, but you are afraid of what he might do."

Anya shot out of her chair. "What are you talking about? What are you people going to do to him?" she asked angrily.

The grandmother shook her fist at Connie.

"Don't you hurt my granddaughter!"

Again Connie held up her hands. "Stop. Just listen. Nicholas will be safe. I give you my word. You need to say these things to start rumors about him. He will need this help from you. Just remember what I have said – he will be safe. I'm sorry but that's all I can tell you."

Anya's grandmother folded her arms and said, "I'm not going. I'm too old to leave here. And, I don't like what this *gypsy* is telling you. Don't go, Anya. Don't trust them." Anya started to cry.

This grandmother is a real pistol, Connie thought as she glared at her. The whole thing is going to blow up because of this stubborn, little, Russian Cossack. Joe told me under no circumstances can I say anything about her son being at the Helsinki airport to meet her. I am supposed to convince them to go without mentioning it in case they are stopped and interrogated at the airport. But, I can't let this "hell-on-wheels" ruin everything.

"Mrs. Kaminsky, you must go." Forgive me, Joe, but I have to tell her, Connie thought. "Your son, Anton, is going to be waiting for you at the Helsinki airport. He knows you are coming, and will be there to meet you."

"Nay, nay," Anya's grandmother said as she put her hand on her chest. "Anton? He is alive? He will be there?" she said softly looking into Connie's eyes as Connie nodded. Then she asked accusingly, "How do you know this?"

"Anton will explain everything to you when you meet him in Helsinki," Connie said.

Anya turned to her grandmother and said, "Enough, grandmother. We are going to do this. Both of us are going to leave and that is final. Now you be quiet and listen to what this woman has to say. And, no more name calling." The grandmother raised her chin and looked at her granddaughter haughtily, "So tell this lady to speak instead of just sitting there then."

Connie spent the next 40 minutes explaining the plan one more time and answering the questions they had.

CHAPTER 39

Monday morning Nicholas came into work. He was sitting at his desk trying to clear off the issues that had piled up while he had been gone last week. "Trying" was a good word, he thought, because I'm a wreck. This was it. After today, my entire life will change. I will never see these people again. But, worst of all, I will never see my beloved country again. Will I even be alive by the end of the day? Has Igor contacted the KGB? What if they are waiting for me outside of the vault? The Americans gave me a cyanide pill to take if the KGB gets to me first. What a nightmare this day is going to be. Have I made the right decision? I can still call this off. I still have time. But, where would I go?

"Why are you here, Comrade? Why aren't you getting the information for the document I told you to prepare?" Igor hissed in Nicholas' ear. Nicholas was so startled. He hadn't even realized Igor had approached him.

"I am going to begin working on the project this afternoon. Right now I need to get these things off my desk. By the way, here is the report the Soviet Command Committee asked you to present," he said as calmly as he could when he passed the paper to Igor.

"See that you start on the document today. Is that clear?" Igor growled as he grabbed the report and walked away.

Nicholas went into the vault in mid-afternoon. He knew he was sweating, but there was nothing he could do about his nerves. The one thing he hadn't anticipated was the intense security check he had to go through at the desk. He had tunnel vision when the security guard told him he had to examine the pen in his breast pocket. He thought for sure they would discover the camera and it would all be over. He fingered the cyanide pill hidden in the cuff of his jacket. But, the guard handed the pen back to him and said, "Sorry, Comrade, but we have to do these things." Nicholas just nodded, unable to speak.

Once inside the vault, the door closed and locked from the outside. In a sense, he was trapped if things went wrong. He began taking pictures of as many documents as he could. The pen was unique in that it worked while he held it as if writing notes to himself. He knew this room was equipped with several overhead cameras to watch every move he made. After more than an hour, he put his pen in his pocket, picked up the notes he had made and walked to the door. He had taken as many pictures as his nerves could stand. Enough was enough. He rang the buzzer to have the door opened by the guard outside.

Here comes the moment of truth, he thought. Is the KGB going to be waiting for me when the door opens? Again he put his hand on the pill.

"All done?" the guard asked when he had the door open.

"Yes, comrade. I am done for the day." He prayed his voice sounded normal as he walked to the guard's desk to sign out.

"Excuse me Comrade, but I have to give you another security check before you can leave," the guard said as he held out his hand for the file Nicholas was holding.

Thank god, I didn't take any hard documents out of that vault, Nicholas thought. At one point, he debated about bringing out an old document he thought wouldn't photograph well. He wouldn't feel safe until this was all over. What have I done? I can still call this off. There is still time.

He arrived at his mother's house shortly after 6:00 p.m. He did not change his clothes, but kept his military uniform on. He waited another three hours until it was almost nine o'clock, then left his house and walked down the street to the neighborhood tavern. He began drinking shots. He met two friends who were matching him drink for drink. They started singing Russian folk songs. The other men in the bar began looking at them as the three got louder and louder. Finally, one of the men told Nicholas they were going to take him home, because he was too drunk. The three staggered out of the tavern as Nicholas tried to make them stay for one more vodka.

Later when questioned by the police and then the hated KGB, the neighbors said they could hear the three men coming down the street singing.

They knew they were drunk because all of them were loud and had trouble walking. The two men, whom they had never seen before, seemed to be having trouble trying to keep Nicholas steady as they walked. Each neighbor interviewed said no, they had never seen Nicholas drunk before. In fact, he was always so quiet. If it wasn't for his car in the street, they would never even know he was home.

"And, when did you hear the gun shot?" All were asked. All reported it was about 15 or 20 minutes after the other two drunken men had left.

"How do you know they left?"

"Because they sang as they staggered down the street away from the house."

By the second morning when Nicholas still had not shown up for work, Igor could stand it no longer. He had to be sure Nicholas had the nuclear documents in his possession before he could contact the KGB. Finally, he sent one of his military aides to Nicholas' house to find out what had happened.

The officer found the front door unlocked and went in. As soon as he had the door opened, the stench of death assaulted him. He had tobreath through his mouth while he covered his nose with a handkerchief. He found Nicholas slumped over a chair in the living room. His face had been shot off. The shotgun was on the floor.

The officer called Igor to tell him it looked like Nicholas had committed suicide. Then he called the police. While he was waiting for them, he began to look around the room. He spotted a hand written note on the table next to the window. He picked up the blood-splattered note and began to read.

I am ending it. I cannot be a part of what Igor has asked me to do. He sent me into the vaults to bring out nuclear documents. I think he plans to sell them to the West. I can think of no other reason why he would ask this of me.

My father was a war hero. I cannot blacken his name by helping Igor sell out my beloved country. This is better. I now leave as a good soldier. I cannot be a part in Igor's plans whatever they are.

The officer folded the note signed by his friend and put it in his pocket. He had worked for Igor for four years and hated every minute of being under his command. He didn't know how to contact the KGB. He would make some inquiries. They had to know about this.

CHAPTER 40

Luck was on Connie's side. Jeff Evans had cabled her while she was returning from Paris. He told her there was a position open in Washington as secretary to Joe Aiello, Head of the Russian Code Desk. It was hers if she wanted it. Monday morning, she sent a cable to Jeff with her acceptance.

Before going into Richard, Connie was sitting at her desk trying to decide what to do. The hard part was going to be coming up with an excuse for Richard as to why she wanted to leave this Friday and not give the customary two-week notice. She decided to just say she needed time back in Washington to unpack and organize her things before she started working for Joe Aiello.

"I have taken the job, Richard. I will be leaving this Friday. I figure there are enough secretaries here at the Embassy. It will be easy to replace me on such short notice." Connie added as she handed the cable to Richard. She was going to add the part about wanting to return early to unpack her things, but Richard spoke before she had a chance.

"Well, you have to do what you feel is necessary. And, you're right, there are plenty of women here to replace you," he said as he handed the cable back to her with a disinterested look on his face.

Ah, Richard. The same hubris right to the end, she thought. I have my excuse ready, but don't need to use it. Big deal. You don't even care. You jerk. I can't get out of here fast enough. She went back to her desk to begin packing.

On Friday the Embassy car dropped Connie off at the Moscow airport for her flight to Helsinki. She had her special Embassy passport and the airline ticket in her hand as she walked to the Customs Gate staffed by Soviet, border guards who worked under the KGB. She timed it so that Anya and her grandmother were five people ahead of her in line. She couldn't believe what a transformation different clothes and a new hair-do could do. Anya's hair was dyed a more platinum blond color now. The people at the Finnish Embassy gave her a Western haircut to go with it. She looked beautiful, Connie thought. Wait until Nicholas sees her.

Anya's grandmother had tints of reddish brown in her grey hair to match the normal Finnish-Baltic look. Connie dared not stare or smile, but it looked like she was enjoying her role of the hard-of-hearing grandmother. She even walked differently. Instead of the usual, stooped, shouldered, defeated Russian posture, she stood straight and tall as she went through Customs. She took on the persona of a middle-class woman. The two of them walked through the gate and into the boarding area without any problem.

When Connie handed her passport to the guard, he studied it for a moment then told her to step out of line as he motioned to another guard.

"Why?" Connie said in English. The new guard took her passport and suitcase. He told her in Russian to follow him. She quickly glanced at Anya. There was pure panic on her face as she looked back at Connie. Connie turned away immediately. Whatever was going on she had to keep the focus on her and off of them.

Nuts to this, Connie thought. You are all going to know I speak Russian and I'm going to do the pain-in-the-ass American act too.

"Hey, what the hell is going on here? I am an employee of the United States Embassy. Just what do you think you are doing?" she asked loudly in Russian.

The guard looked surprised when Connie spoke Russian, but he did not answer her. He unlocked the door to a small room and told Connie to go inside. He put her suitcase on the table and told her to unlock it.

Connie leaned across the table and shook her finger at the guard. "I want you to call the attaché at the American Embassy and get him here right now. His name is Alan Young. How dare you subject me to this? Do you want to start an international incident?"

I don't know if hassling an Embassy secretary would qualify as an international incident, but it sounded good, she thought. And, why the heck are they hassling me? Oh, Anya. Please be safe.

When Connie unlocked her suitcase, the guard removed all of the items in it and began to examine each of them closely. He opened all bottles and smelled the contents. When he was through, he took out a knife and began cutting the lining and examined the inside.

"Hey, you stupid ass. What the hell are you doing?" Connie yelled. The guard sneered at her and made a wider cut.

Oh, oh. I better cool it, she thought. This is getting scary. What the heck is going on?

When the guard was done with his examination, he headed for the door. He had his hand on the knob as he turned back to Connie. "You wait here. And, no telephone calls," he said rudely in Russian as he walked out.

Holy moly. She felt her knees begin to weaken and had to grab onto the table to steady herself. She stood leaning against it for a few moments while taking in deep breaths of air. Then to get back to some sort of normality, she pulled the suitcase over and began throwing her things back into it with one hand while still holding on to the table with the other. Thank goodness, the State Department ships most of our stuff. I only have to take this carry-on, she thought as she closed it.

The guard returned and handed her passport back. Then he said Connie was free to leave. No explanation. No nothing. Just, she was free to go. Her first instinct was to start yelling every curse word she could think of at him. But, then common sense took over as she silently snatched her passport back and picked up her suitcase. But, she did give him a dirty look as she walked to the door.

When she opened it, there he was – Ivan the Weird, the KGB agent from Paris. He was staring at her with a mixture of pure hatred and smugness. He's letting me know he is the one behind this. This is payback time for what I did to him in Paris. I think I am going to faint. Please God, let me be safe, Connie prayed. It's just me, no one from the Embassy to help. She continued to walk as calmly as she could to Customs. Am I going to be shot in the back? Does he know about Anya and her grandmother? Did he pull them off the plane? Is that also part of the payback? These things flew through her mind as she handed her passport to the guard for the second time. I have got to get on that plane to make sure they're safe.

This time the guard stamped her passport, but sneered at her as she proceeded into the boarding area. Her immediate reaction was to start running to the plane. But, this was Moscow. If I did that, I would be stopped again for sure, she thought as she walked as fast as she could without drawing attention to herself. "Let me make it. Let me make it," she whispered as a mantra with every hurried step she took. She was less then 30 feet away, as the Finnair representative began closing the ramp door.

"No," Connie shouted. Then she did begin to run. The hell with it, I don't care if I am causing a scene. I need to get on that plane!

"Wait! Please, wait!"

The representative saw Connie coming and stopped with the door ajar. "Please hurry, Madam. You are very lucky, the plane is just about to take off," the man said as Connie whizzed past him down the ramp.

She continued to run, while saying, "Thank you" to him. Then she shouted to the personnel who were beginning to shut the outer door of the plane. Startled, they stopped closing the heavy door. Connie didn't wait until they got the door fully opened. She just turned sideways tugging on her suitcase to get it through the door with her. The startled stewardesses had to get out of the way as she wedged herself through the door. The passengers stared at Connie as she proceeded down the aisle. Trying not to stumble, she looked around frantically for Anya and her grandmother. Six rows back, there they were. All three looked relieved as they spotted each other. Connie put her suitcase in the overhead and took her seat.

She took a moment to say a quiet prayer. "Thank you, Lord. I promise never to sin again. Well, I probably will sin, but I am going to try awfully hard not to." She leaned back in her seat and closed her eyes. Ivan the Weird, you dummy. You were so intent on getting your revenge on me. Your actions kept Anya and Joe's grandmother safe. But, it's not over yet. We are going to be in Soviet airspace for all but about 30 minutes of this four and a half hour flight. The Soviets have been known to make planes turn around and return while still in their airspace. And, even for the last 30 minutes in freedom, I can't acknowledge Anya for fear there is KGB on board. They would think nothing of killing Anya as she left the plane in Helsinki.

What kind of life have I gotten myself into, she thought. Never being safe. Never trusting anyone. What a dreamer I was to think this would be exciting and glamorous. Do I really want to continue to work for the CIA?

It seemed the entire plane relaxed when the pilot announced the plane was out of Soviet airspace. When they landed, Connie entered the terminal and stood to the side to wait for Anya and her grandmother. She wanted to make sure Joe's father was there to meet them. If not, she would call the Embassy for help.

As soon as the two of them exited through the door, a man rushed up and hugged them. She knew it was Joe's father, because he looked like an older version of Joe. She stood to the side not wanting to intrude on their reunion. When Anya saw Connie standing there, she raced over and hugged her and kept saying thank you. Even the grandmother came over to her. She didn't hug Connie or say thank you, but she did hold her hand while tears streamed down her cheeks.

CHAPTER 41

Earlier that week, late in the evening an old-looking woman finished her night job cleaning offices. She was on the streetcar returning home to the poorer section of Moscow. Actually, the woman was only 39 years old, but she led such a hard life that the years took their toll. When she got off the streetcar, the woman wrapped her threadbare coat around her to ward off the cold and slowly walked to her apartment. It had been four days since her drunken husband was gone. And, she prayed he wouldn't return tonight either. She was sick of the beatings and the constant rages. In the four days he had been gone, even the children had begun to smile again. They weren't living in fear. She hoped he was dead. He had a low-level job in the Russian mafia. He hardly made any money. What little he did make, he spent on vodka. They would be better off without him, the woman thought.

She climbed up the five flights of stairs to her apartment and unlocked the door. In the dim light, she could see there was an envelope lying on the floor just inside the door. She stooped to pick it up. After closing the door, she opened it.

"Dear God in Heaven," she whispered. There were one thousand rubles in it. With her fingers shaking, she counted it five times to make sure. She clutched money to her chest and began to weep.

"How is this possible?" she whispered. Then, she checked the apartment to make sure her husband wasn't there. He can never know about this money. I have to find a good hiding place for it. Her mind started racing. She could finally buy warm blankets for the children and pretty bows for the girls' hair. But, she had to be very, very careful how she spent the money, only a very little at a time. Here in the Soviet Union, if people knew you had money, it meant you stole it. And, you would be reported.

In the middle of that same week, the man awoke with a raging hangover. He felt like he was as close to death as he could get. Last night he blacked out before getting to the end of the second bottle of vodka. He woke up in his clothes and didn't even remember how he got home from the tavern. He thought he was going to throw up on the street-car as he went to work. The people around him all smelled. They reeked of body odor and bad breath. He got off one stop early, because his stomach could stand it no longer.

He was the Medical Examiner at the Government Morgue. He was late for work. By the time he entered the building, he didn't feel any better and he was furious. Then when he walked into the morgue, he was hit by the fetid smell of a decaying body.

"Who the hell brought that in here," he roared pointing to the corpse on the gurney. "Get it out of here now."

The assistant lab technician cringed when he heard him. He knew his boss had a hangover and was going to take it out on him yet again. Reluctantly, he entered the room.

"Comrade, this is Nicholas Gregorovich, a suicide who was brought in early this morning. We have orders from General Igor Polakova of the Army to check dental records and fingerprints to confirm the man's identity," the assistant said as he handed the papers to his boss.

"I don't care who ordered the damn confirmation. Get this thing out of here right now," the man yelled as he grabbed the papers from his assistant. Then, he made the mistake of looking at the corpse lying on the table inside of the unzipped black bag. When he saw maggots eating at the face, he leaned over and threw up.

The lab assistant hurriedly grabbed the gurney, pulled it out of the room and wheeled it down the hall to the back entrance. To hell with this, he thought as he zipped up the bag. He wasn't the one who was going to sign the identification. He left the body on the back loading dock and went back in to call the mortuary.

The medical examiner opened his desk drawer and removed a bottle of vodka. He wiped his mouth after he took a large swig of liquor and waited until he felt some relief. Then he sat down at his desk to sign the document.

"Those military pricks think they are so important," he mumbled. "They think they can order everyone around. To hell with it." he roared. "I'm not touching that stinking body. You want a confirmation, Army big shot? There, you've got it. The guy is Nicholas Gregorovich," he said as he signed the paper with a flourish.

Igor couldn't be happier to learn his stepson had committed suicide. Finally, I have gotten rid of the bastard forever, he thought as he left his mistress, Helena's flat that evening. He had wanted to wait to contact the KGB until he was sure Nicholas had taken documents out of the vault. Even though he badly wanted to set him up for treason, working with Mislav Boginin could be so dangerous. Now he didn't even have to do that. The idiot had killed himself. Problem solved and no KGB, he smiled. And, this was a good night with Helena too.

As he came out of her flat, he was thinking about all the things she had done to him that night. He was so engrossed in his sexual fantasies he didn't see the young student until he bumped right into him. The student was carrying books and folders that scattered and fell to the sidewalk.

"You stupid pig," Igor shouted. "What the hell's the matter with you?"

"Sorry, Comrade, sorry," the student said as he began gathering his things.

"Oh, sorry, Comrade. This is yours," the student said as he handed a folder to Igor. Igor shoved it back at him.

"This isn't mine, you shit-head," Igor sneered at the young man. Then he realized the student was a Jew. "A Jew. A stinking, lousy Jew," he roared. "Get out of my sight before I have you thrown in the Gulag, you piss."

Igor was so angry he didn't see the man holding the camera standing across the street in the doorway. The man took pictures just as both the student and Igor had their hands on the folder. Later when the film was developed, the face of the student would be replaced with the face of Isaac Libowitz, a high-ranking Mossad agent.

The student quickly gathered his belongings and hurried down the street.

CHAPTER 42

Late on Wednesday afternoon, a battered, work truck was slowly grinding up the slight grade of a small hill in Romania.

"I sure hope this thing gets us all the way to the Bulgarian border," David Levi said as he shifted down to first gear.

"It's a Soviet truck," Nicholas said as he looked over at David and shrugged his shoulders. "I'm surprised it went this far without breaking down. If it does break down, I'll run the rest of the way to the border. I have got to get out of these stinking clothes. I think there are bugs in them." He began scratching his neck. "How could that guy wear these clothes? Was it really necessary for me to wear his old rags? Couldn't I have just changed into some of my own work clothes."

"No. You didn't have anything this old to match your new identification papers." David answered.

After a moment, Nicholas asked, "Did you really kill him?"

"We had to in order to make it look like your suicide. We blew his face off while he was wearing your uniform." Nicholas sucked in his breath. Even though he was military, he wasn't used to this type of ruthlessness.

"But, don't shed any tears for that *shtarker*. He was a real piece of work," David added. "He worked for the Russian mob in the Jewish pogrom. He got his kicks beating up Jews just for the hell of it. You don't even want to know the things he did to our young girls . . . and boys. The world is much better off without him. Trust me on that." David looked at Nicholas with sad eyes.

"I'm sorry, David." Nicholas said before he turned and looked out the window at the countryside. He became lost in thought.

"You know I couldn't believe a Jew was going to help me get out of the Soviet Union. I still can't understand why the Americans passed me off to you. For all the things we Russians have done to the Jews, why are you helping me?"

Once over the hill, David put the truck into fourth gear. "Yeah, well, just to let you know helping a Russian doesn't sit well with me either. I'm not doing this for you. I'm doing this for Connie. If it wasn't for her, I wouldn't be here at all."

"Connie?" Nicholas said. "Who the hell is Connie? Is that a code name for this whole operation?"

David looked at Nicholas with contempt. "You don't even know who she is, do you? What a *putz* you are. Your handler never told you the whole story, did he? All right, once we get onto Greek soil, I'll explain why I am the one getting you out. But, not now."

"In case we are caught. If I am tortured, the less I know, the less I can tell, right?" Nicholas shook his head.

"That's the game, sonny boy." David knew about the murder of Nicholas' father by his stepfather. Because of the murder of his parents and sister, he could identify with Nicholas as to why he did what he did. But, at the same time, he had little sympathy for him. It was the stinking Russians who armed the Arabs who were killing the Jews.

The truck made it into Bulgaria the next day. David and Nicholas wiped it clean of fingerprints and then ditched it in a town located in the middle of the country.

"It will probably be striped by tomorrow morning. Good. Nothing to leave behind," David said as they walked away toward the bus station. They bought food from various small stores on their way. If they bought too much food and spent too much money in only one store, the Bulgarians would become suspicious. And, there was always some weasel sucking up to the Communists who would report them.

They took a bus as far south as they could go, about 40 kilometers from the Bulgarian/Greek border. They arrived in the small town in the late afternoon. It was situated in the foothills of the mountains. Since it was winter, even here in the South, the sun was beginning to set early. So they could start for the border immediately.

Now came the hard part. In order to get over those low-lying mountains during the night, they had to walk about four kilometers an hour just to reach the border. The mountains weren't high. But, trying to keep a pace of just a little over two miles an hour could prove impossible. Once they got over the mountains, they had to get across a wide valley to reach to border's edge. Once over the border, they then had to cross a river on the Greek side in order to reach Greek soil.

"Look, Nicholas, if we can't make the whole trip tonight, we will hide out in the mountains and wait until tomorrow night to try again," David said as they began walking up a hill going south. "We're both young and in good shape, but, neither of us has trained for this walk."

"I understand, David. But, let us try to do this tonight. I have come this far. I just want this over. I want the fear to go away." Nicholas picked up the pace.

At three o'clock in the morning, they were lying flat on top of the last ridge looking down into the valley at what lay before them. Giant searchlights swept across the land at timed intervals. At the rim of the lights across the valley, they could see the bank of the river on the Greek side. David stared across the valley at two tall trees on the other side of the Greek river and waited.

"How the hell are we going to make it the rest of the way?" Nicholas was exhausted. After that grueling trek up and down the mountains, he didn't think he could go any farther.

"There – there's our signal," David whispered as he pulled out a small flashlight. He turned it on and off quickly twice. He knew the Soviet guards were situated in bunkers located on either side of them and wouldn't see his light flashing straight out. The narrow beam of light across the river blinked once and then went out. Hopefully, the guards did not spot that light. It had been blinking for one second once every hour since midnight. It would not be turned on again now that contact was made.

"Listen. We are going to wait here for an hour. We will watch the searchlights and time them. See if the guards alter their sweep. We can finish the remainder of our food. And, the rest will do us good. Now that we have made contact with the men across the river, they have orders to wait no matter how long.

After the hour's rest, both of them felt they could continue to go on. Even better, it was now the darkest part of the night. They had another two hours of the deep darkness before the sun would start making an appearance on the horizon.

The sweep of the searchlights had not changed. They would not be in any danger while they worked their way down the side of the low-lying mountain, because the path of the lights only swept the valley below. The biggest danger wasn't being caught in the searchlights. By counting the sweep intervals, they knew they would probably have the time to get across the valley if they hurried. The biggest danger was going to be not stepping on the landmines planted in the valley. David had shown Nicholas a map he had that indicated where the mines were placed. They studied it while they were driving here.

"Okay, let's go," David whispered. Nicholas nodded. They went as fast and as quietly as they could down the side of the last foothill. They fell flat on the ground behind a large boulder and waited until the searchlight made another sweep past them and was now receding. Then, they got up in crouched positions and began to run in a single file across the valley. David was in the lead. They kept their eyes on a tall tree near the river and ran straight toward it. Per the map, it was the path free from mines. They had approximately two and a half minutes to cover one hundred yards.

They were twenty feet from the barbed wire fence when the searchlight began coming back. The grass and brush was a little over two feet high where they were running, but a few feet up ahead the growth had been bulldozed all the way to the fence. Still in the tall grass, David made a split second decision. No way could they get through the fence before the light would be directly on them.

David turned and whispered as he threw himself on the ground. "Get down, and don't move." Nicholas was so intent on running he didn't hear David. By the time he reacted, he had to go down on the grass along side of him.

"Don't move a muscle," David hissed as the light moved over their bodies. It took a full five minutes for the light to complete its sweep and then recede. "Comrade, be very careful where you put your right hand. Look at your hand. You are only centimeters away from the top of a land mine."

Nicholas looked down and thought his heart would stop. "Let the light make another sweep, David. I don't think I can move right now." He slowly inched his hand away from the mine.

After the second sweep, now composed, they rose once again and made it to the coiled barbed wire. David took a wire cutter out his jacket. He flipped on his back and began cutting the wire overhead as fast as he could all the while sliding farther under it. Nicholas followed him crawling on his stomach as he slipped through the opening David made. The light was coming back now. It would reach them in seconds, but the river was only a few feet away from the edge of the wire and the light barely shone on the Greek riverbanks.

Once through, David got on his knees and pulled Nicholas through the coil. Then they ran to the river, jumped in and sank down in the cold water with only their heads above water. The shock of the cold water coming from the mountains made them both want to gasp. But, neither made a sound as they waited for the light to recede again.

"There they are," David said with relief as the rowboat came across the river. The two men in the boat helped them up and had blankets ready.

ZINGER #1

Two weeks after Nicholas and David had made it safely out of the Soviet Union, a MI-6 agent from the British Embassy, entered a small park on the East side of Moscow. He was carrying a copy of the newspaper, *Pravda*, under his arm. When he sat down, he looked around as if he were waiting for someone. At one point, as he started to put the newspaper down on the bench, an envelope slid partially out. The agent hastily put it back inside the paper and quickly looked around to see if anyone had seen the mistake. He began tapping his heel in a nervous gesture as he kept checking the two entrances to the park. He also looked at his watch several times.

The CIA agent entered the park from the right. As soon as the MI-6 man spotted the American, he raised his chin in a nod; stood up; left the newspaper on the bench and quickly walked out of the park in the opposite direction.

Before proceeding to the bench to retrieve the newspaper, the CIA agent bent down to retie his shoe. While down, he scanned the people in the park. That's when he spotted the KGB agent rapidly approaching the bench vacated by the MI-6 agent. The KGB agent snatched up the newspaper and walked out of the park, but not before he turned and smirked at the CIA agent.

The CIA agent, still on one knee, lowered his head and banged his fist on the ground. He rose and quickly left the park.

Two hours later, Joe Kamisky skidded to a stop at the gate of the British Embassy. The KGB agent assigned to watch the Embassy was standing across the street. He saw Joe park his car; slam the door as he got out; and storm up to the building. The agent noted he had a furious look on his face. He wrote down Joe's behavior in his notebook.

Once inside, Joe was escorted to the Office of MI-6. The agent, who had been the one in the park, met him at the door.

"It went perfectly, Nigel. The KGB took the bait. And, to add some spice, I just put on a little show for the Russian across the street as I came in here." Joe smiled at his counterpart and shook his hand. "Thanks, for your help."

"I can't tell you how much fun this was, Joe. I practiced for two hours at being a bloody screw-up before I went out. Then, the first time I laid the newspaper on the bench in the park, the bloody envelope wouldn't move. I had to pick it back up and give the paper a shake and try it again. I thought for sure I had blown it on that one, and the KGB would figure out they were being played."

"Oh, and here's something that will make you laugh," Nigel chuckled as he led Joe into his office. "On my way to the park, the bloody KGB tail lost me! I had to double back and find the bloke so he could pick me up again. Can you believe these idiots? You owe me one for that, Joe."

"Tell you what, Nigel. You can come to the American Embassy for dinner. I'll have our chef make you a big plate of fish and chips."

"Ah, manna from heaven, old boy. By the way, when do you think you will be getting the copies of the nuclear documents to pass along? The boys in London are anxious to get a look-see. Thanks for giving us a head's up on them."

"I still can't figure out the Mossad role in all this, Joe. How the hell did they even get into the Soviet Union?"

Joe's CIA agents and the Israelis were the only ones who knew about Gregorovich's escape. All the other agencies believed they were helping Joe nail Polakova. He did not want any mention of Gregorovich known. And, just as importantly, as a professional, he was too humiliated to have any of his colleagues know about Richard Morgan's refusal to help in the defection

"It's been a hectic few weeks, Nigel. When we're two, old retired agents sipping rum drinks on a Caribbean Island, I'll tell you all about it. But, in the mean time, thanks again for your help."

The envelope retrieved from the park landed on Mislav Boginin's desk shortly in the early afternoon.

He studied the contents. There was a picture of Igor Polakova handing a folder to a man. Attached to the picture was a handwritten note from MI-6 to the CIA.

One of our agents shot this photo of Polakova and Isaac Libowitz. Word has it he sold out to the Mossad. Sorry, old chaps. I know you Yanks were trying to work with him on the nuclear stuff. My guess is you didn't offer him enough money. Better luck next time.

Mislav Boginin sat absolutely still. His hands were balled into fists. He had never been so angry in his life. He knew with a certainty he was going to kill Igor Polakova. The only question was how much pain was he going to inflict before he did.

All Soviet borders were staffed by guards under the command of the KGB. Not only was Polakova a traitorous pig. His actions were the direct result of this Mossad agent slipping into the Soviet Union right under the noses of the KGB. He was sure the Brits and the Americans were having a good laugh right now. Igor made Mislav look like an inept fool. And, that was something he could not forgive.

That night, he had Igor picked up on his way home from work and brought to the KGB safe house in Central Moscow. Before Mislav said one word to Igor, he slapped him across the face so hard that Igor fell out of his chair. He told his two agents to stand him up and hold him. Then Mislav beat Igor, again, and again, and again. When Igor lost consciousness, Mislav still wouldn't stop hitting him. His two agents finally pulled Mislav away from Igor. They had never seen their boss so out of control before. Mislav's chest was heaving as he looked down at Igor's bloodied face.

"Get some water and bring him around. Let me know when he's able to talk," he said as he left the room.

When Igor was coherent again and seated back at the table, Mislav began his interrogation. He produced the suicide note left by Nicholas; the picture of Igor handing over the folder to the Mossad agent; and, the note from MI-6 to the CIA. Igor kept denying everything. He maintained his innocence.

"You are a traitor, Igor Polakova. Do not lie to me," Mislav roared.

Then Mislav reached into his pocket and pulled out an old, yellowed piece of paper, unfolded it and laid it on the table in front of Igor. It was the letter Igor had sent to Stalin many years ago accusing Nicholas father of homosexuality and his plans to have him killed.

"Oh, by the way. We found something interesting when we searched Gregorovich's house. It was hidden under the carpet."

"My, my, Comrade. Your cunning puts the KGB to shame," Mislav said with a sneer.

Because he was so badly beaten, it took a moment for Igor to be able to focus on the paper in front of him. His brain took even longer to process what he was reading. It wasn't until he got almost to the end of the note that he realized it was the letter he, himself, had written. Somehow, Nicholas had found it. How? Igor was in such pain. It was so hard to think. Slowly, slowly the idea took shape.

"He did it," Igor whispered through swollen lips. "He set me up. Nicholas set me up for what I did to his father." Igor began to cry now. He turned and grabbed Mislav's arm. "Get him," he said frantically. "Find him. He'll tell you. He set me up. This is all his fault."

Mislav took the revolver out of his holster and held it at his side. "We can't get Nicholas. He's dead, Comrade. But, you're not, you traitorous bastard." He raised the gun, pulled the trigger and put a hole between the eyes of Igor Polakova.

"Get rid of this scum. Make sure he is never found. I will deal with his superiors," Mislav told his agents as he returned the gun to the holster.

ZINGER #2

Joe informed Richard Morgan that Nicholas had gone over to the Mossad when he found out the CIA wouldn't help him defect. He had no intention of telling Morgan the agreement between the CIA and the Mossad or any of the things the other agencies did to help Joe pull this off. He leaned across Richard's desk. "If you had allowed us to get him out, this wouldn't have happened."

But, Richard wasn't about to take the fall for this. He blamed Joe. "You're the one who screwed this up. You're the one who told him the truth, you idiot! You should have told Gregorovich the CIA would have helped him then we would have gotten our hands on those nuclear documents. Now the CIA has nothing, because of the poor job you did."

"And, a lot you know, Kaminsky. You have no proof Gregorovich went go over to the Mossad. He committed suicide," Richard looked at him with a superior sneer on his face. "I read the report from your night agent."

Joe slammed his hand on Richard's desk. "Didn't you hear anything I told you? If we took the documents without trying to get him out, no one would have trusted us again. We would have tarnished our reputation not only with our contacts, but with all the other spy organizations. All of them would be reluctant to work with us again." Joe shouted in exasperation.

"Who are you kidding?" Richard asked. "None of the other agencies or Russian contacts even knew we were working with Gregorovich. We could have had those documents in our hands right now. If the KGB learned about it, so what? They simply would have killed Gregorovich. And, that would have been the end of it."

"That's precisely why Gregorovich committed suicide, Richard. He didn't want to be killed by the KGB. And, what I can't seem to get through to you is, if the KGB had learned about Gregorovich, they would have told the entire world the CIA left him out to dry," snapped Joe.

"I'm going to write you up on this one. This screw-up is going on your record in Washington," Richard shot back.

Richard smiled as he thought back on the conversation with Joe. He didn't have to worry about putting a spin on Joe's write up. In fact he didn't even have to bother writing him up, because Joe had been called back to Washington one week ago.

Good riddance to that smug know-it-all, Richard thought. When I have the big corner office in the White House as advisor to the President, Joe can come in and clean it.

Joe was back in Washington sitting in Jeff Evan's office at the CIA building. Jeff did not look pleased as he stared across his desk at Joe. This was the first time the two had ever met face-to-face.

"All right, Joe. You want to tell me exactly why I got a call from the Mossad informing me they have Nicholas Gregorovich . . . and the nuclear documents? That's all we need, one of those hotheaded Middle Eastern countries getting their hands on the formula for the nuclear bomb. The CIA can never allow that to happen."

Joe tried to keep the stare with Jeff while he figured out how to explain this. But, in the end, it was Joe who blinked first. He slowly blew out a breathe of air and looked out the window. His mind was racing. He had heard about Evan's exploits as a field agent during the Second World War. This wasn't someone you could bullshit.

Finally making up his mind, Joe turned back to Jeff. "All right, here's what happened." He spent the next 45 minutes laying out the facts.

"Why didn't you contact me here in Washington when you knew Richard wouldn't sanction the defection?" Jeff asked dumbfounded.

"There wasn't time, Jeff. We only had a five-day window. Gregorovich contacted us *after* Igor had told him to go into the vaults. It was the first time he mentioned defecting. And, I definitely didn't want to risk the possibility of the Soviets picking up his name, encoded or not, in any of our messages. You and I both know the Embassy is surrounded by listening devices."

He was quite sure he was going to be fired for going behind Richard's back. The CIA does not tolerate rogue agents. But there was one more assignment he wanted to do before they let him go.

"I want to ask you to let me do one more thing, Jeff. Let me escort Gregorovich back from Israel to the U.S. for his debriefing here."

The powerfully built military raft landed on the shore of Israel at midnight. The two sailors shut the motor down and pulled the raft onto the sand. Joe Kaminsky stepped out of the raft. Other than the lapping of the waves, all was quiet on this remote coastal beach.

"Sir," said one of the sailors. "I hope you understand the U.S. Navy is breaking military law by landing this craft on foreign soil. If we're caught, we'll be put in prison; and, the Navy will do nothing to help us."

"I understand," Joe replied. "But, we will not be here that long. As soon as we pick up our passenger, we will be out of here. And, I have a feeling the Mossad has told the Israeli Army to look the other way for the next hour. "

Joe scanned the road to the north and spotted a car coming. It stopped when it reached the area where Joe was waiting. Two men got out of the car. The moon was out, so Joe was able to see that it was David Levi and Nicholas Gregorovich who hurried down the beach toward him.

"Welcome to freedom, Nicholas," Joe said in Russian as he put his arm around the other man's shoulder.

"Well, I still don't know what total freedom is, since I have been kept in a safe house for the last two weeks; but, at least I am not scared anymore," Nicholas replied.

"Nicholas, go with these two sailors. They will get you into a life vest. We will have a long trip back to the waiting aircraft carrier. I need to speak with David for a moment."

"Don't worry, Joe," David said after Nicholas went with the sailors. "I'm sure you already know that the Mossad called your CIA agent at the U. S. Embassy here in Israel to be present when we developed the pictures of the documents Nicholas brought out. And, we gave the pen to your agent when we were finished. By the way, that pen is fantastic. You wouldn't mind sending us a box of those. We would put them to very good use."

Joe chuckled. "I'll see what I can do. We have to hurry and get out into international waters, David. But, before I go, I wanted to ask you a question. What are you going to do about Connie?"

"What do you mean? Did she say something about me," David asked quietly.

"Oh, Levi. Who are you kidding? I saw the way you looked at her when we were in Paris. And, no she didn't say anything about you. But, I also saw the look on her face when we left your apartment. So, Romeo, are you going to do something about that?"

"Yeah, I think I am going to do something about that," David said as he smiled at Joe.

Two weeks later, Richard Morgan was called back to Washington. He hoped it was for a reassignment. He hated Moscow. But, he thought it was odd that Jeff Evans wanted to meet him at the Washington Hilton and not the CIA building. Jeff was waiting for him in the lobby when he arrived from the airport.

"I've got a room reserved here where we can talk, Richard," Jeff said as he pointed to the bank of elevators.

Once in the room, as Richard was walking to a chair next to the window, Jeff said, "Don't bother sitting down, Richard. What I have to say won't take long."

"You're through, Richard. As of this moment, you no longer work for the CIA. The personal things in your office and apartment in Moscow have been packed up and are being shipped to your home in Providence."

It took a few beats before Richard could even respond. "What? What are you talking about, Jeff?"

"I'm talking about Gregorovich and your refusal to help him defect. Because of your lack of judgment, he went to the Mossad with the nuclear secrets before he committed suicide." Jeff wasn't going to tell Richard anything about the Mossad handing over the documents and the fact Gregorovich was alive and well and now with the CIA here in the U.S. That information was classified. And, Richard didn't work for the CIA anymore.

"That is absolutely not true, none of it. I was the one who wanted to get Gregorovich out. It was Joe Kaminsky who wouldn't do it. He said he didn't know how he could get him out," Richard answered frantically. "And, besides, there is no proof Gregorovich went to the Mossad. He committed suicide."

Jeff slowly shook his head in disgust. "Two things, Richard. I wouldn't bother trying to show your face in Washington for a long time. All doors will be closed to you here. And, whatever thoughts you might be entertaining about your father-in-law helping you, forget them. The DCI already called him and explained exactly why you are being let go." Jeff turned and walked out of the room.

ZINGER #3

"1968, the beginning of a new year . . ." Connie whispered as she stood at her apartment window gazing out at the snow gently falling on Washington D.C. A Sarah Vaughn record was playing softly in the background.

It's so quiet in here. Oh, how I've needed a time like this ever since I got back. She closed her eyes and let the peace of the moment envelop her.

So much has happened this past year. I think I lived one whole lifetime in just the last six months alone.

Even though Richard finally got fired, it's still difficult for me to think about all that happened between us.

I received my very first marriage proposal from a guy who lives six thousand miles away. Just my luck . . . I wonder where the relationship would have gone if David and I lived near each other and had a chance?

I lost my boss. "You're still in my thoughts, Tom," she whispered. "I wish you were still here to share all these things with me."

Never in a million years did I think I would be involved in plans to help three people escape from the Soviet Union. When I look back, it's like I am viewing it in the third person. That couldn't possibly have been me. Joe said the CIA brought Anya to Washington so she and Nicholas could be together while they were debriefing him. Well, it was actually Nicholas who said he wouldn't say a word to them unless he saw Anya first.

And, per Joe, his grandma was driving Joe's mother and father nuts with her meddling. I can just imagine. I wonder if she called Joe's mother a "gypsy" yet. Just the thought of her makes me smile.

The CIA debriefing I had to go through two weeks ago when Joe was here. Ugh. That was horrible. Once Joe told Jeff everything that had gone on, I was pulled in and questioned for the part I played. I didn't expect that. Those guys didn't miss anything either. Once I mentioned David's name, they wouldn't stop asking questions about him; when did I meet him; how did I meet him; how many times did I meet him. I hope I was right when finally just I started from the beginning when he came to Washington. It must be okay, because I still have my job. And, Joe, who was so worried he was going to lose his job, is now back in Moscow. Jeff told him he was too valuable to lose. I'm glad for him.

Joe said because of me, the CIA was now going to look into hiring women agents. Pretty cool. But, I have no intention of applying for the job. I don't ever want to be as terrified as I was at the Moscow airport. I have to laugh at all those spy novels I collected over the years; and, all my plans to be the famous spy. How glamorous. How exciting. How awful this business really is in reality.

Connie was pulled out of her reverie when the buzzer to the lobby door sounded.

"I wonder who that is? It's nine o'clock at night," she said to herself as she pushed the buzzer.

"Connie? It's me David Levi. Buzz me up."

"David?"

He just stood there in the hall when she opened the door to her apartment. "I told you I would come here when it was all over." A few flakes of snow were still on his jacket and in his hair.

"Marry me."

Connie was stunned. Then she broke out in a smile. "Oh, David," she chuckled and slowly shook her head in amazement. "Come on in. Let's talk."

David took off his coat and Connie hung it in the closet. She took a seat on her sofa, but David walked across the room and stood at the window.

He looked out at the city as he began speaking. "I was serious when I told you I would come here. I want to marry you, Connie. I knew it the first time we met here in Washington."

"I'm tired. So tired," he said softly. "Every time I set foot in Israel, the memories come back."

"I want peace and happiness and love. I want to come home every night and smile. I don't want to be alone anymore. I want to share my life with you. Can you understand what I'm saying?" he said as he turned and faced her.

"I understand, David," Connie said quietly. "But, we live six thousands miles away from each other. How will we ever have a chance to know if we should even be together?"

"I quit the Mossad, Connie. That life was not for me. I know that now. It didn't help to exorcise my memories. And, I really do have a degree in Agriculture. I want to be a farmer. That's all I've ever wanted to be. I'll go anywhere in the world with you. I'll even raise tulips in Holland, if that's what you want," he said with a smile recalling the first time they had met.

Connie stood, walked to the window and put her arm around David's waist. "You know, David, I have had an idea floating around in my head ever since I got back from Moscow. I'm really not cut out for the CIA either. I've been thinking about getting a teaching job at a small college somewhere. Maybe, getting away from this crazy, secretive world of ours will give us the time we need to know one another."

"I'd like that," David replied as he put his arm around her shoulder.

"Ah, you wouldn't want to kiss me would you, David?"

He looked at her and smiled. "Thought you'd never ask," he said as he took her in his arms and kissed her. It was as electric as they both remembered.

She slowly pulled away and took his face in her hands. "Given time, I think we are going to work out just fine," she said as she looked up at him.

"Good. I'm glad," David replied as he held her in his arms. "Oh, I almost forgot. Aaron Zucker asked me to give you something," he said as he pulled an envelope from his inside jacket pocket and handed it to Connie.

"What is it," Connie asked as she slipped her finger along the flap to open it.

"I don't know. He just told me to be sure to give it to you."

Connie removed a single photograph and looked at it with a puzzled look on her face. After a moment, she said, "Oh, no."

She laughed as she handed the picture to David. "It's a picture of Aaron Zucker's seven grandchildren!"

EPILOGUE

The three retired couples were sitting at the Captain's table waiting for him to arrive. They were on a boat cruising on the Volga River from Moscow to St. Petersburg and had been invited to dine with the Captain on their first night out. Five of the six people were old friends who had worked together over forty years ago. Between the three couples, they had seven children and thirteen grandchildren. The smart phones were passed as they shared pictures of their families.

All carried United States passports, but only Connie Levi, nee O'Rourke, and Joe Kaminsky were actually born in the U.S. David Levi and Joe's wife, Marisa who was from Slovenia, became U. S. citizens when they married. Nicholas and Anya Gregorovich received new names and U. S. identities when they defected. Their names were now Donald and Nancy Kummer.

They kept in touch during the years, quietly at first. Then with the break up of the former Soviet Union, they met openly at least once a year. This was the first time any of them had been back to Russia.

"So, Don, how was your excursion into the city of Moscow today?" Connie asked the tall grey-haired former Russian man. "Did you get lost?"

"I didn't get lost, but how things have changed. I kept looking for familiar landmarks. Most of them are gone," Don replied in English with just a hint of a Slavic accent.

"Don and I went to the café where we first met. Guess what? It is now an electronics store! Can you imagine? During Soviet times, no one was even allowed to own a typewriter for fear of subversive writings. And, now anyone can buy a computer or smart phone and communicate with the entire world," Nancy added enthusiastically.

"Did you get to see your mother's house, Don?" Joe Kaminsky asked.

"Yes, and thank God it is still there. I don't know what I would have done, if it had been torn down. We drove passed. So many memories," Don added reflectively. Nancy reached over and squeezed his hand.

"Just think of our children and grandchildren, Don. And, how blessed we have been," she said softly. He smiled at his wife.

Joe's wife, who married him after he left the former Soviet Union, turned to him and asked, "So what about you and Connie? Has the city changed for the two of you?"

"Well, it certainly is cleaner and seems more cosmopolitan, right?" He looked at Connie for confirmation.

"You're right. That's a very good description of how Moscow has changed. Cleaner and more cosmopolitan," Connie said. "Joe, I'm assuming you didn't have any trouble with your Visa. Do you think this new government, still knows who we worked for when we were here?" Connie asked.

"Actually, my Visa came though in the usual time. But, the border guards at the airport looked at my passport longer than they should have. So, I just leaned heavily on my cane and coughed like the old man that I am. That seemed to appease them; and they let me in. What about you David? Any trouble?"

"Not really, but you see, I was never *officially* in the Soviet Union back then," David said as he shrugged his shoulders. "I doubt I'm on any watch list here."

After a short while, the Captain arrived at the table. "I apologize for being late. I had a few last-minute instructions for my crew," he said as he pulled out a chair and sat down.

The waiter immediately came and filled their shot glasses with vodka. He did not fill a glass for his Captain however.

The Captain raised his water glass to them. "Well, a toast to new journeys and old friends." The six of them joined the Captain and raised their glasses.

"I think this is the first time I ever met a Russian who didn't drink vodka," Don said.

The Captain smiled slightly and looked some-what embarrassed. "Ah, yes. I can understand why you would think that. My, ah . . . my father was a very mean alcoholic. When he drank, he beat my mother and sisters and me. I just made a vow never to drink."

"I'm sorry, I shouldn't have pried. I apologize," Don said.

"Well, actually, my story is not so sad. My father disappeared in 1967 when I was only ten years old. So the beatings stopped and my sisters and I have had a good life. My oldest sister is a doctor and lives in Tallinn, Estonia. My youngest sister plays the cello in the Moscow Symphony and has traveled around the world. Here, let me show you something," said the Captain as he reached into his pant's pocket and pulled out some rubles. He spread the rubles in front of his dinner plate. There were five in all.

"Our mother gave these to us. Two months before my mother died in 1989, she called my sisters and me home and told us about our father. He was a member of the Russian mafia. She said that she didn't know why or how he disappeared. His body was never found. But, she thinks the mafia must have killed him, because about three days after he disappeared, my mother found an envelope containing 1,000 rubles that had been slipped under the door to our apartment."

Connie took in a breath of air and opened her mouth as if to speak. Under the table, David quietly put his hand on her thigh and gave a gentle squeeze.

"My mother was so scared," the Captain continued. "Although, we needed the money just to survive, back then in Soviet times, if anyone had money, you were immediately reported to the authorities. If she began to spend too much money, people would think she stole it from her work as a cleaning lady. She knew she could not lose her job. So over the years, she ever so slowly spent only a few rubles at a time. In 1989, when she called us home, she still had fifteen rubles left and gave each of us five. For the passed eighteen years, I have carried these rubles with me."

The Captain was lost in thought for a moment as he looked at the coins spread out on the table. He shook his head as if to clear his mind. "It's strange, I don't normally tell people this story. I don't know why I did tonight," he said as he picked up the rubles and returned them to his pocket.

By this time, Joe, who was sitting next to Connie, had his arm on the back of Connie's chair. He leaned over and whispered in her ear.

"Not a word."

"But, Joe, he needs to know . . ." she whispered as she looked at him questioningly.

"Not . . . one . . . word," he responded.

BIOGRAPHY

Jackie Granger has had an eclectic life. She was a baseball coach, Brownie leader and lunchroom mother when her four children were young. She went back to college, earned a degree in Accounting and was a C.P.A. In between her career in Corporate Tax Departments of financial institutions, she served in the Peace Corps as a business consultant in the former Soviet Union country of Latvia. Currently, she lives in a small town in Wisconsin to be near four of her seven grandchildren.

Made in the USA
Columbia, SC
17 November 2020